HIGH-OPP

HIGH-OPP

Frank Herbert

WordFire Press
Colorado Springs, Colorado

Published by
WordFire Press, an imprint of
WordFire Inc
PO Box 1840
Monument CO 80132

ISBN: 978-1-61475-038-3

First Trade Paperback Edition: April 2012
Printed in the USA

www.wordfire.com

Foreword

Even at the beginning of his writing career, Frank Herbert wrote whatever inspired him, irrespective of genre, market, or audience tastes.

His first novel, *The Dragon in the Sea*, was published by Doubleday in 1955 and bought outright by Universal Studios for film (the movie was never made). A tense science fiction war drama set aboard a futuristic submarine hauling fuel through enemy lines — the story focused on the pressures encountered by the crew when faced with insurmountable dangers, a science fiction spin on *Das Boot*.

With his family on the road in Mexico, Frank Herbert tried to eke out a living as a writer (as described in detail in Brian Herbert's Hugo-Award-nominated biography *Dreamer of Dune*). He followed up *Dragon* with a succession of manuscripts, novels and stories of all types: thrillers mysteries, science fiction, mainstream.

None of them could find a market.

But he was determined and followed his creative vision with tale after tale, all of which remained unpublished. Among them were *A Game of Authors, We Are the Hounds,* "Paul's Friend," "Wilfred," "The Waters of Kan-E," "The Yellow Coat," "Public Hearing," *High-Opp*, and many others.

Undaunted, Frank Herbert penned books and stories . . . until he wrote the most unpublishable novel of all, a massive SF epic called *Dune*, which was rejected more than twenty times before being released by an obscure publisher of auto-repair manuals. *Dune* went on to become the best-selling SF novel of all time.

High-Opp is a dystopian novel about high society and low society, a story that would prove oddly prescient about today's class-warfare debates. Daniel Movius, a successful bureaucrat who scores high in the public opinion polls that drive society, is betrayed and finds himself stripped of everything, cast down to the dregs of society — which he discovers are ripe for revolution.

This lost work is now being published for the first time anywhere.

—Kevin J. Anderson

Chapter 1

People averting their faces as they walked past the office door finally wore through his numbness. Daniel Movius began to clench and unclench his fists. He jerked out of his chair, strode to the window, stared at the morning light on the river.

Far out across the river, in silver layers up the Council Hills, he could see the fluting, inverted stalagmites of the High-Opp apartments. And down below them, the drabness, the smoke, the dismal carpet of factories and Warrens.

Back into that? Damn them!

Footsteps. Movius whirled.

A man walked past the door, examined the blank opposite wall of the corridor. Movius raged inwardly. *Sephus! You son of a Sep!* A woman followed. *Bista! I'd as soon make love to a skunk!*

Yet only yesterday she had made courting gestures, bending toward him over her desk to show the curves under the light green coveralls.

He hurled himself into his chair, sent the angry thoughts after them, the words he dared not use. "Avert your faces, you clogs! Don't look at me!"

Another thought intruded. In Roper's name, where was Cecelia? Was she another averted face?

Two men appeared in the doorway pushing a hand-cart loaded with boxes. Movius did not recognize them, but the LP above their lapel numbers told him. Workers. Labor Pool rabbits. But now he was one of the rabbits. Back into the LP. No more special foods at the restricted restaurants, no more extra credit allowance, no Upper Rank apartment, no car, no driver, no more courting gestures from such as Bista. Today, he was Daniel Movius, EX-Senior Liaitor.

One of the workmen at the door coughed, looked at the desk plaque which Movius had not yet removed. "Excuse me, sir."

"Yes?" His voice still held its tone of command.

The workman swallowed. "We were told to move the Liaitor files to storage. Is this . . ."

He could see the workmen's manner change. "Well, if you'll excuse us, we have work to do." The men came in with an overplayed clatter of officiousness, banging the handcart against the desk. They turned their backs on him, began emptying files into boxes.

Stupid low-opp rabbits!

Movius finished dumping the contents of his desk drawers into the wastebasket, topped the pile with his name plaque. He saved only a sheet of pale red paper. The message chute had disgorged the paper onto his desk less than an hour ago, as he'd been sorting the morning mail.

"Opinion SD22240368523ZX:

"On this date, the Stackman Absolute Sample having been consulted, the governmental function of Liaitor is declared abolished.

"The Question:

"For tax economy reasons, would you favor elimination of the supernumerary department of Liaitor?

"Yes: 79.238 percentum.

"No: .647 percentum.

"Undecided: 20.115 percentum.

"May the Majority rule."

With motions of thinly suppressed violence, Movius folded the paper, thrust it into a pocket. "For tax economy reasons!" They could get a yes-opp matricide for tax economy reasons!

One last look around the office. It was a big place, scaled for a large man, an orderliness to it under the apparently random placement of desk, filing cabinets, piled baskets of papers. There was a smell about the room of oily furniture polish and that kind of bitter chemical odor found in the presence of too much paper. It was a room with an air of dedication and no doubt about it. Dedication to quadruplicate copies and *the-right-way-of-doing-the-job*.

Movius noted that his phone had been dislodged from its cradle beside the desk. He replaced it, ran a hand through his stubble of close-cropped sandy hair, unwilling now that the moment had come, to say goodbye to this space in which he had worked four years. The room fitted him like an old saddle or like the body marks in a long-used bed. He had worn his grooves into the place.

Low-opped! And with so much unfinished work. Bu-Opp and Bu-Q were going to be at each others' throats before the month was out. The government was damned soon going to find out it had need for Liaison. The bureaus were too jealous of their domains.

Damn them!

He stared at the workmen. They had cleared two files, were emptying a third. Movius was ignored; another discard to be stored away and forgotten. He wanted to fling himself on the men, knock them into a corner, scatter the papers, wreck things, tear things, destroy. He turned and walked quietly out of the office, out of the building.

On the front steps he paused, his eyes seeking out his parking slot in the third row. There was Navvy London, the driver, leaning against the familiar black scarab shape of the car. THE CAR—a primary token of authority. Sunlight shimmered on the flat antenna which spanned the curving roof. Movius looked up to the left where the scintillant red relay ship hovered above the spire of the prime generator, sending out its invisible flagellae of communication and energy beams from which the city sucked its power.

He wished for the strength to hurl all of his pent-up curses at this symbol of authority. Instead, he lowered his eyes, again sought out the car, that tiny extension of the relay ship. Navvy leaned against the grill in his characteristic slouch, reading a book—one of those *inevitably* deep things he *always* carried. The driver pulled at his lower lip with thumb and forefinger, turned a page. Movius suspected that some of Navvy's books were on the contraband lists, but the man was the kind to carry it off. A look of youthful innocence in his brown eyes, a wisp of black hair down across his forehead to heighten the effect. "A contraband book, sir? Great Gallup! I didn't think there were any more of those things drifting about. Thought the government had burned them all. Fellow handed it to me on the street the other day when I asked what he was reading."

Seeing Navvy brought back a disquieting thought: How had Navvy known about the low-opp? How did a Labor Pool driver get official information before it became official?

Movius slipped between the First Rank cars, the Second Rank cars, slowed his pace as he approached the relaxed figure of the driver.

Navvy sensed Movius' presence, looked up, pushed himself away from the car. His young-old face became contemplative. "Now do you believe me, sir?"

Movius drew a deep breath. "How did you know?"

The contemplative look was replaced by casualness. "It came over the LP grapevine."

"That's what you said before. I want to know how."

"Maybe you'll find out now that you're an LP," said Navvy. He turned toward the car. "Anyplace I can take you? They haven't assigned me yet. They're still upstairs wrangling over who'll get my carcass."

"I'm no longer privileged, Navvy. It's forbidden."

"So it's forbidden." He opened the rear door of the car. "They know where they can put their forbiddens. One last ride for old time's sake."

Why not? thought Movius. He shrugged, slipped into the car, felt the solid assurance of the slamming door. Navvy took his place in front.

"Where to, sir?"

"The apartment, I guess."

Navvy flicked the power-receiver switch, turned to back the car from its slot. Movius watched the concentration on the man's face. That was one of Navvy's secrets, a power of concentration, of storing up. But what about the other secret?

"Why won't you tell me *how* you came by the information?"

"You'd only accuse me of being a separatist again."

Movius felt a humorless smile twitch at his lips, remembering their conversation that morning on the

way from the apartment. Navvy had said, "Sir, probably I shouldn't be talking, but I've word they're going
to low-opp you today."

It had been an ice-water statement, doubly confus-
ing because it came from his driver, someone like an
extension of the car.

"Nonsense! Silly scuttlebutt!"

"No, sir. It's over the grapevine. The question was
put on the eight o'clock."

Movius glanced at his watch. Ten minutes to nine.
They almost always were passing the Bu-Psych Building about this time. He turned. There was the grey
stone pile, early workers streaming up the steps.

A question on the eight o'clock? Movius could picture the returns ticking into the computers—Shanghai,
Rangoon, Paris, New York, Moscow. . . . The Comp
Section, working at top speed, could have results in two
hours. It was impossible that anyone could know the
results of an eight o'clock before ten. He explained this
fact to Navvy.

"You'll see," said Navvy. "Those autocratic High-
Opps have you picked for the long slide down."

And Movius remembered he had chuckled. "The
government doesn't function that way, Navvy. Majority
opinion rules."

What a trite set of mouthings those were when he
thought back on them. Right out of the approved history books. Right out of the Bureau of Information
blathering. But these thoughts brought a sense of un-
easiness. He twisted his lapel, looked down at the pale
mauve and white of his coveralls, code colors for
Tertiary Bureau heads. All of his clothes would have to
be dyed. He fingered his identification number on the
lapel, the red T stitched above the number. That would

be ripped off, LP replacing it.

Labor Pool! Damn them!

Penalty service could scarcely be worse.

The car was climbing through the privileged section now, Gothic canyons of silvery stone interspersed with green parks. There was an air of seclusion and reserved quiet in the privileged sections never found in the bawdy scrambling of the Warrens.

Movius wondered if the word already was out to his apartment manager.

Chapter 2

The Bureau of Psychology had a special suite of rooms atop its building on Government Avenue, fronting the river. In the forenoon, the ledges outside the office windows were a roosting place for pigeons which watched the riverbanks and the streets for signs of food. A flock of them strutted along the ledges, cooing, brushing against one another. The sound carried through an open window into one of the rooms.

Two walls of this room were taken up by charts covered with undulant squiggles in colored inks. In the center of the room, spread out on a table, was another chart bearing a single red line, curving, dipping, ending in the middle of the sheet like an uncompleted bridge. A white card rested on this chart near the red line's terminus. One corner of the card was weighted by a statuette of an obscene monkey labeled "High-Opp." A strictly subversive, forbidden statuette.

Three people occupied the room—two men and a woman. Or, rather, they *inhabited* the room. They seemed fitted to it by an attitude of absorption. One got the feeling they had been initiated into the secrets of this room through a deeply esoteric ritual.

Nathan O'Brien, chief of Bu-Psych, stood up, closed the window to shut out the noise of the pigeons. He returned to his chair at the end of the table. O'Brien was a ferret of a man, who wore his Top Rank black with an air of mourning. He had the reputation of possessing a photographic memory, was conversant with seven of the pre-Unity languages, and was said to have a giant library of forbidden books of the ancients. Things were rumored of him that one would expect to hear about a man whose position could command privacy. There was about him a sense of remoteness, as though thoughts passed between his greying temples that no other men could fathom.

Quilliam London was a snorter. He snorted now, meaning he had been about to get up and close the window himself. Damned pigeons! He did not sit his chair, he *rode* it as though it were on a pedestal or a podium. Quilliam London had once been a professor of semantics before such teaching was low-opped and a heavy penalty put on infractions. Now he was on the retired rolls, serving an occasional afternoon at his district infirmary, filling out treatment cards, or visiting Nathan O'Brien at Bu-Psych, an activity carried out quietly. He was a rail of a man with the face of an eagle and hunter's eyes. His seventy years were carried as though they were fifty. Thin wrinkles down his cheeks, thickening veins and greying hair gave him away, however, as did a tendency to be short of temper when talking with anyone under thirty.

Grace London, Quilliam's daughter, turned away from the window where she had been watching the pigeons. She had rather enjoyed their cooing and was sorry when O'Brien closed the window. She was a woman with too much of her father's thinness of face to be beautiful and people often were disconcerted by her habit of turning a piercing stare on whomever she addressed. There was youth in her, though, and the kind of sureness which comes with health and vitality. It gave her a sparkle, a crispness which some men found attractive.

"I believe he's the man," said O'Brien. He nodded toward the chart on the table.

"That's been said before, Nathan." His voice rumbled.

"But this time there's a higher probability," said O'Brien. "Look at his sorter card. Loyalty index ninety-six point six. Intelligence in the genius range. His decision chart is around here somewhere. Six questionables in twelve years."

Grace London moved restlessly along the table, following the red line on the cart with a finger. "What does Cecelia say? Is he another Brownley?"

O'Brien looked up at her as though she had interrupted a thought. "She says not. She's been watching him four years now, and her opinion is pretty trustworthy. We've just run a Malot-final on him from her completed reports. It's uncanny how closely he fits the classic requirements."

"I'm being overly cautious," said Grace. "Brownley was such a disappointment." She moved the monkey statuette to a more central position on the chart.

"Brownley was a result of poor timing on our part," said O'Brien. "We were too eager."

Quilliam London scratched his chin with his thumb. "That high loyalty index could backfire on us. With our treatment, Movius might turn it inward, go all out for number one."

"That's the chance we take," said O'Brien. "Even if that does happen, he'd be useful to us up to a point. We could get rid of him, blame his death on . . ."

A door behind him opened and a blond man

stepped into the room. "Chief, Cecelia Lang called. Movius just left her apartment. She says everything went off as planned."

O'Brien straightened. "Get moving, Grace. You have to beat him to the Warren. I'll have supply rush a make-up kit down to the car. You can change on the way." He brushed a hand through his thinning hair. "Wouldn't want Bu-Con recognizing you out there and asking questions."

She nodded, followed the blond man out the door.

Quilliam London arose like a folding ruler being stretched to its limit. "I'd best be getting along, too. Has Marie Cotton been warned to look out for Movius?"

"She was in yesterday," said O'Brien. "She had a relayed report on Warren Gerard and the latest Bu-Trans maneuvering."

"That's a funny thing about Gerard," said Quilliam London. "What prompted him to send those specifications through the sorter at this particular time?" He pointed to the card on the table. "Gerard is going to be surprised when he finds out who his specifications fit." He rapped a knuckle against the chart on the table. "This Movius is encouraging. I'll have a long talk with the man tonight, see if he measures up to his psych card and to Navvy's judgment."

"He had better be right," said O'Brien. "We don't have time for another wrong move like Brownley."

Chapter 3

Navvy let Movius out of the car half a block from the apartment. "You understand, sir. No sense rubbing their noses in it."

"Yes. Good opps, Navvy." Movius stood a moment on the curb, watching the car grow smaller, finding it difficult to realize that had been the last ride. His watch showed almost eleven. He turned, hurried toward the grill and glass front of the apartment building. In the lobby there was an atmosphere of refined gloom, thick carpet underfoot, a whirring of air-conditioning fans.

The manager had been notified. He darted across the lobby as Movius entered. "Oh, Movius?"

Now it's just plain Movius, he thought. It used to be Mr. Movius. *That glorified janitor!*

"You no longer live here, Movius." The manager's face reminded him of a rabbit, a particularly gloating rabbit. "I have your new address right here." He handed Movius a narrow strip of paper torn from a notepad.

Movius glanced at it, read: "Roper Road, 8100-4790DRB." A Warren! Well, he'd expected that. DR for downstairs rear, B for bachelor. No tick rug in the lobby there; bare to the hard tiles. No isolation there; turmoil. A Warren.

The manager stood looking at him, obviously

enjoying his discomfiture. "Your effects already have been moved."

Already moved! he thought. Scarcely two hours and already moved. As though they wanted to cover him up, like an unsightly mistake.

"Was there any mail for me?" asked Movius.

"No, but I believe there was a tele-message on the printer. Just a moment." He walked around a corner, returned with another piece of paper.

The note was brief:

> *Dan,*
>
> *Just got the word. Comp Section still needs good hands. We could put through a special request – Phil Henry.*

Movius put the note in his pocket. Phil Henry. How long had it been? With a feeling of guilt, Movius realized he had not seen Phil Henry for almost a year. He remember the bushy-browed eager look of the man when they'd worked together back in Comp. Almost a year. Movius shook his head, turned to the manager.

"Is Miss Lang in her apartment? I'd like to see her."

"Miss Lang?"

The anger came out in his voice. "Yes, Miss Lang. She wasn't at work. I'd like to know if she's home."

"I'll see if Miss Lang wishes to see you," said the manager. He went into his cubbyhole. Movius heard him talking on the phone.

One of the privileges of Upper Rank quarters, thought Movius. No unauthorized visitors. Ergo: he had to ask permission to visit his fiancée. He wondered what would happen to her now. Probably a quick shift into another section. Only the top felt the heavy blow of a low-opp. Trained underlings were always needed somewhere.

The manager spent a long time on the phone, finally emerged, grinned at Movius before speaking. "You may go up." The grin was a positive smirk.

Movius went to the elevator, punched for the thirty-third floor. Why hadn't Cecelia been at the office? She seldom failed to report on time, often rode down with him. Movius thought of all the effort he had put out to get her this apartment next to his, the favors he had promised, the extra credits spent. And Cecelia only a twelfth ranker. That had made it difficult.

The elevator stopped, the door snicked back. Movius turned left, passed his own door, 3307, saw it was open and a cleaning crew working inside. The urge to pause and have a last look around the rooms swept over him. But he couldn't face the thought of explaining to the cleaning crew, accepting their smiles of superiority. He turned away, noticed two men loitering in the doorway opposite '07, Cecelia's apartment. One of the men looked familiar. He had seen the fellow somewhere. The two men showed interest in Movius as he knocked on Cecelia's door. One moved across the hall, hand in pocket. "Just a . . ."

The door opened, revealing Cecelia—chic, blonde, wearing dress coveralls the color of her hair. Her mouth was startling with a wild orange lipstick. The effect was a gold statue come to life.

Movius stepped forward to take her in his arms, ignored the man behind him. "Cecie, I . . ."

She put him off, extending her right hand as though for him to kiss. With her other hand she waved away the man in the hall. "Dan, how nice you could come by. Come in, won't you? I've a guest." She took his hand.

There's something wrong with her voice, thought Movius. He said, "Who was that in the hall?"

"Nobody important; come along." She led him into the apartment.

A wide-bodied man with crew-cut iron-grey hair and a face like a square-hewn plank stood up from the couch. He was putting a handkerchief into a side pocket. The handkerchief showed orange stains the color of Cecelia's lipstick. Movius paused. Now he knew the reason for the men in the hall. Bodyguards. This was Helmut Glass, Coordinator of All Bureaus: The Coor. Although the directors of the top bureaus shared nearly equal powers, this man was titular head of government, the top of the pyramid.

"Sorry about your job," said Glass. His left eye squinted, the muscles of the cheek rippling with a nervous tic. "I just heard about it a couple of hours ago."

On the tip of Movius' tongue was the urge to say, "Then my driver knew it before you did." But his thoughts skipped a beat. It was now eleven o'clock. Two hours subtracted from eleven left nine o'clock, about the same time Navvy had been making the prediction. The Coor could not have known two hours ago unless his information came from a source similar to Navvy's or from foreknowledge. But how could he predict the Opp?

"Just about two hours ago," repeated Glass. "I was shocked."

He's emphasizing the point, thought Movius. It's a calculated lie. And how could Glass be shocked at the knowledge? He and the other top bureau chiefs — Com-Burs — had framed the question. *The man wants me to lose my temper*, thought Movius. He wants me to call him a liar. *Sorry, Mr. Glass.*

In an even tone, Movius said, "That gave you just

enough time to get over here and comfort Cecie, didn't it?"

The Coor's eyes widened, narrowed. "Cecelia . . ." He turned toward her.

Cecelia stepped to one side, said, "Helmut has transferred me to his department. Isn't that lucky? Now I won't lose my apartment."

Not *The Coordinator has transferred me* . . . Isn't this cozy? And dear Helmut received a big kiss when he made the announcement.

Glass put a lighter flame to the cigaret, looked at Movius through a blue cloud of smoke—distant, untouchable. "We can always use a good secretary. When I heard your department was low-opped and Cecelia out of a job, I snapped her up." A streamer of cigaret smoke blew toward Movius. "Don't know what we're going to do about you, Dan. Something will probably turn up, though." Again the tie rippled the Coor's cheek, squinted his eye.

So it's Helmut and Cecelia, thought Movius. He looked at Cecelia, wondering how he could get her away alone to talk to her. Something about the way she was looking at him—half laughing, superior— reminded him of a fact buried far down in his memory. Cecelia Lang had been engaged to another man once. What was the fellow's name? Brownley or something like that. He'd been the head of the now defunct Department of Antiquities and had gone out and gotten himself into one of the penalty services for failure to report the discovery of an ancient library. And now that he thought about it, Movius recalled that Cecelia had been transferred to Liaison the day after what's-his-name Brownley was low-opped.

Looking at Cecelia with her cream-washed skin and

eyes he could never see past, Movius thought, *I inherited her.*

He said, "I was wondering if I could see you tonight."

A perfectly formed look of disappointment came onto her face. He had the sudden disquieting picture of Cecilia practicing that look before her mirror. "Oh, I'm sorry," she said, "but Helmut has asked me . . ."

"Tonight is Summer Festival," said Glass. "Had you forgotten? Cecelia said you hadn't asked her; so *I* invited her."

It wasn't what they said nor even their actions—taken singly. It was a combination of things more subtle than gross perception is accustomed to noting. Movius felt a wall descend between himself and these two. So this was how Brownley had felt. *Sorry, Brownley. I didn't know.* For a moment, Movius failed to recognize the feelings inside himself—the tension like hunger. Then he knew it—hate, a boiling hurt, struggling for expression. He thrust his hands into his pockets, clenched his fists.

"You do see, don't you?" asked Cecelia. Again that vague hint of superior laughter.

"I see," said Movius, startled to find his voice high-pitched. Glass looked up sharply, smiled. "I'll be going now," said Movius.

Cecelia turned away. Glass grinned at him, insolent, assured. Only the tic, briefly touching the man's cheek hinted at something less than assurance.

Movius whirled, almost ran from the room, not seeing, moving by memory. He was in the Common Transport headed for his new address in the Warrens before he could calm his nerves.

Without using a word that could be challenged,

Cecelia had just given him the gate. He recognized that she had done the job with a masterful touch. It was typical of her, typical of the way she had always handled him, holding him a tantalizing arms-length away even after they were engaged.

A maddening woman. And what did he really know about her? The name—Cecelia Lang. The lovely, enticing body. But he didn't know that except from looking at her and longing. Many men had enjoyed that privilege. What else did he know about her? Now that he put it to the question, he realized there was a little else he *knew* about Cecelia Lang. She had never talked about her parents except to say that once her mother had possessed the morals of slum goat. Maybe she'd never known her father. From all Cecelia had ever said about herself, she might well have started life at the age of twenty-one. Or perhaps at nineteen. He seemed to remember hearing somewhere that she'd known Brownley two years. *Brother Brownley.*

Chalk up another averted face; a lovely, cleverly averted face. Cecelia Lang.

His new address was so far back in the Warrens of the river flat that the Transport was almost empty when they neared it. Movius watched the corner numbers, stood up when they passed 8,000. A man's voice whispered hoarsely behind him, "I'll bet he has a cute little LP out here he doesn't want his driver to know about."

Movius became acutely conscious of the color of his clothing, the T above his lapel number. Even without these things he knew there would be something in his manner to brand him High-Opp. How long would it take for that to wear off?

The Transport stopped. Movius stepped down. Forty-seven was four blocks away along a curving street filled with screeching LP children who grew quiet as he approached, stared silently as he passed. An occasional woman sat on a doorstep staring at nothing. Where the privileged sections rarely heard loud noises, quiet was the exception here—until the workers came home and fell into weary sleep. Even then sounds filtered through the night: giggles, screeches, curses. And the smell. A fetid notice of unwashed closeness. Movius walked through it as though in a dream, hearing his heels click against the concrete, remembering his childhood in a Warren such as this, conscious of the eyes which followed him.

It was a building like all the others—lifeless windows and a door like a gaping mouth. A Warren. How long had it been? Eleven years? No. Twelve years. Great Gallup! Twelve years! Since the day he'd made the Calculation Corps, that breeding ground of the middle ranks. That was where he'd met Phil Henry. They had been two eager beginners. Eager to learn. Eager to believe anything good about a system which gave them this tremendous opportunity. He wondered how much Phil Henry still believed. Then there was Phil's offer. The Computer Section; it was only four stages above LP and fourteen ranks from the top. A few privileges. Better housing. Pride held him back, the memory that he'd not seen Phil for almost a year, had ignored an old friend. Yes, Phil was a friend. No face averted there. Later on he'd look up Phil. Not now.

A thought came back to him: Comp Section, fourteen ranks from the top. Had he been aiming for the top? He realized with a shock that something in him had been doing just that, something unconscious and driving. And all the while his conscious self had moved along placidly like a passenger in a commuter tube deep under the earth.

A gang of children raced between Movius and the Warren, ran off down the street shouting.

There was the Warren. *His* Warren. He was back to the beginning now; nothing to do but wait until his various talents went through the sorter, came up with an open job. That took time. Maybe a month; maybe more. He didn't look forward to wearing the LP's on his lapels, having old acquaintances appear not to notice. Well, inside then; off the streets.

He found room ninety, paused outside the door. He could picture it, identical to the one in his memory — seven by nine feet, narrow bed, standard bedding, a bathroom three and one-half feet square (shower opposite toilet, washbasin under shower, just enough room to stand erect), beside the bathroom a closet of the same size. Three and one-half goes into seven twice and seven feet is the Opinion-prescribed width of a standard bachelor room. The plastic walls with their memorized pipes and conduits subtracted perhaps three-quarters of an inch.

May the Majority rule!

Movius opened the door, drew back when he saw a strange woman sitting on the bed, a small grey mouse of a woman with sallow complexion and hair drawn back tightly in a worker's bun. "I'm sorry," he said. "I thought this was my room. The door . . ."

She jumped up, held out a sheet of paper, said, "Darling, I couldn't stay away any longer. I had to see you."

This is a joke, thought Movius. He noted a stack of Transport Department moving boxes in a corner, one on the bed. His?

"Please come in. Don't be mad at me." She beckoned to him frantically.

Movius put down the briefcase, closed the door. The click of the door roused him and he started to re-open it. She shook her head violently, waved the paper at him. "Darling, what's wrong?" she demanded. "Are you tired of me already?"

He moved forward, accepted the paper, read it. The words took a while coming through because the woman went on rambling about her passion for him and the cruelty of men. It was neat block printing; "Do not say a word aloud. We may be overheard. You are in terrible danger. Come to the bed, pretend you are making love to me."

When she was certain he had read the entire message, she grabbed it from him, crammed it into her mouth, chewed it and swallowed it with a convulsive gulp. She took his hand, dragged him to the bed, put her mouth close to his ear. "Say something, you fool," she whispered. "Don't you know what to say to a woman?"

He found the anger inside him where shock had hidden it. More people pushing him around! He jerked her to him, hissed in her ear, "Who are you? What's the meaning of this?"

"I'm Grace London, Navvy's sister. He sent me as soon as he found out. Pay close attention. You're to be transferred to the Arctic Labor Pool for weather survey."

Her eyes made him uncomfortable, staring at him so queerly. This obviously was more grapevine poppycock! But he remembered the accuracy of Navvy's other prediction. It was as though the thought opened a door on the Arctic, letting in a blast of icy air. "That's penalty service," he whispered, subdued. "High mortality."

Roper's name! Had they read his angry thoughts?

"Oh, darling, I'm so happy you're not mad at me," she said. "Kiss me again." She made a low smacking around with her lips, bent and whispered, "It will be discovered too late. A big mistake. So sorry. Eulogies for poor dead Mr. Movius. Posthumous restoration of rank."

A dead High-Opp, he thought. Her mood of urgency began to creep through his numbness. He muttered, "Darling, I've missed you, too." He moved to make the bedsprings squeak, whispered, "Why?"

"No time for explanations," she whispered and blushed as he again squeaked the springs. "Do exactly what I say. After I've gone, wait for darkness, then go out and catch a Commerce Transport. Ride it to the end of the line and go into the Carhouse. Find Clancy in the office. He'll give you the keys to his locker, a change of clothes and instructions where to go from there." She squeezed his hand, said in a loud, clear voice, "Darling, why don't you come to my place tonight? This is too open here." The springs protested as she stood.

Still in a semi-fog, he arose, watched her open the door, glance up and down the hallway, duck out.

The air held the charged feeling of static electricity after she had gone. As the mood of it melted away, he felt let down, unsure. *Pop-mag pap!* he thought. Who'd want to spy on a bachelor room in a Warren? And that nonsense about the Arctic Labor Pool. Mistakes like that just weren't made.

But he had been low-opped. And the official question, when put to closer scrutiny, appeared to have been phrased toward that end. "For tax economy reasons!" But who would want to spy on . . . Then he remembered. A privilege of the top five ranks was an apartment in a building where freedom from spy beams was maintained by a master scrambler on the roof. A High-Opp phone could not be tapped for the same reason. He'd been living away from this sort of thing for too long. Bu-Con was always spying on the Warrens, looking for Sep activity.

Movius cleared the box off the corner of his bed, lay back. Navvy had sent his sister. Sometimes drivers were unaccountably loyal. He'd had more freedom than most drivers, too. Birthdays off, personal trips. Now, maybe Navvy was returning the favor.

The bed felt hard, uncomfortable beneath him, more like a gymnasium mat than a bed. Gymnasium! He'd lost his privilege card for the gymnasium. No more sessions on the mat with Okashi, no more steam baths, no masseuse. No more of anything that had made his life bearable. They'd even take his library permit for the reserved stacks. Back to the apathy of the Warrens.

What have I come to? he wondered. Climbing up through the bureaus and departments was enough once. The competitive game. In fact, as he thought about it, that was all there had been. Pay attention to the game, live by the rules, *believe* the rules. Looking at his world now was like awakening after the loss of a pair of dark glasses which had obscured his vision.

Cecelia and Helmut!

He pounded a fist against the bed until it hurt. Cecelia had been an expensive trinket, a badge of office.

The Red Slip. Opinion SD22240368523ZX.

Almighty Opinion!

The full import of his loss began to come through to his consciousness. He caught himself sighing, felt like a shell vacuumed of everything but weary resentment.

Navvy had sent his sister. Navvy was right this

morning. *Is he right this time? What am I going to do?* The question conjured up a vision of Movius' father. "Never ask *what* you're going to do, son. Ask *how* you're going to do it." Ah, yes. His positive father, full of history, discipline and good intentions gone astray. A history teacher in an age which sought to forget its own past, living out his life as a common laborer in the LP Warrens, ladling the knowledge of remembering contraband books into his son.

His father had started him on this road. The old man had died when Movius was twenty, the year he'd made the Calculation Corps. He couldn't remember his mother. She had died in the educator purges. "The people must have a scapegoat, Dan. Give them their own knowledge to fight. Laugh while they destroy their salvation!" That was his father again; his father in the bitter mood, showing the growing son how to adopt protective coloration: "Act dumb when you're with the dumb; act smart when you're with the smart. But never act more intelligent than the man above you."

The old man had taught too well.

Movius twisted on the bed. Damned low-opp mattress!

Where had it all begun? Ah, the history books again, the forbidden, hate-provoking history books. Low-opped all! It had started in the Twentieth Century with polls to predict the outcome of the crude elections of that era. Sampling methods were improved for almost a century during which emphasis on the sample poll became greater and greater.

Then along came Julius Stackman, born in the Twenty-First Century, following the wars which ended in world government. Stackman and his queer mind which linked a series of electronic relays into the

Brownian Movement Regulator. Absolute random.

Give the machine a job: Supply a nine-digit code number for every responsible adult of age sixteen or over. Next, select three numbers. Every person in the world with those three numbers repeated in his code and in that series step up to a registration kiosk. Give code number, name and thumbprint. Click, click, click, click. *Answer the question, please.* If you don't register and answer and you haven't an adequate excuse, off you go the Arctic Labor Pool or the Sewer Maintenance Gangs. Who wants to be in the ALP or the SMG? Better to get up from your sickbed, answer the question. Register your opp.

Unless you happen to know somebody in the Very-High-Opp.

"Bill was with me. Official business."

You might also know somebody in the Seps, too, who could get you a rubber stamp of your thumbprint. Then a friend could register your opp. But this method wasn't well known.

Give the machine a job!

"What would be an absolute formalization of randomness?"

Out of this came the Mathematics of Impellation, reducing the so-called "laws of chance" to a set of usable factors and reducing the correlative error in a sample-poll to something negligible.

All of this from the square root of minus one.

And more, too. For a time there was a boom in small hand computers for games such as chess. The computers showed the optimum move under any set of conditions. With both players using them, it became evident that the person making the first move always won. A few purists barred the computers, but they were always running into flashy winners with hidden computers. Interest died. Almost fifty years passed before the invention of a new type of game based on Rorschach cards. The ink blots elicited strictly personal reactions under which the rules of the game changed. Formalization was loose. Some people still played these games. Nathan O'Brien of Bu-Psych was an expert.

They gave the machine the job and the machine became the government.

There developed around the poll-taking function a hierarchy of bureaus—The Bureau of the Census (Bu-Sen), The Bureau of Opinions (Bu-Opp), The Bureau of Questionnaires (Bu-Q), The Bureau of Control (Bu-Con), The Bureau of Information (now Bu-Blah even in its own halls), The Bureau of Psychology (Bu-Psych), The Bureau of Transportation (Bu-Trans), The Bureau of Communication (Bu-Comm) and on top of the pyramid, The Bureau of Coordination (The Bureau).

All were handmaidens to the Stackman Selector.

Not to mention Com-Burs, the committee made up of the chiefs of the twenty-five top bureaus. Com-Burs framed the questions. Bu-Q passed on the questions. BIG RUBBER STAMP. Bu-Opp filed away the answers which were then laws.

May the Majority rule.

Always spell Majority with a capital M.

Strange how the top jobs became family property. Helmut Glass was the fourth of his family to be The Coor. Occasionally he stepped down for another bureau chief, allowed the man to serve a year. Even The Coor has to have a vacation.

At the Bureau of Communication, in a small room just under the transmission tower, a man would punch out the code numbers and question.

"Code 449:

"Is compulsory teaching of any subject an invasion of privacy?"

A straightforward question. Speaks right out like a man. But look at those pushbuttons: "compulsory" and "invasion of privacy."

"No man's going to tell me to do something I don't want to do!"

Tick, tick, tick, tick, tick into the Computer Section of Bu-Opp. Yes, yes, yes, yes, yes, yes, yes, yes, yes, yes, yes, yes, yes, no (kick out his number for investigation; lotta Seps around Paris), yes, yes, yes, undecided, yes, yes . . .

File it away in the master retainers. It's a law now. *Opinion RE40407770877TX: No education subject may be compulsory.*

Compulsory teaching of Semantics? Low-opp!

"Well then we'll just offer the classes for whoever wants them."

Semantics teaches that words can dispose a man to think in a certain manner, that they can compel his thinking. Low-opped.

"We'll set up a counseling service: How to Keep People From Influencing You."

This is Semantics under another name. Negative compulsion. Low-opped.

Sixty-one thousand new recruits for the penalty services. A few escaped by public denunciation of their teachings. Quilliam London was one of these. When the carefully prepared riots came, his wife and older daughter did not escape.

Side effects crept into the system — forced conformity. If the Majority rules, there must be standardization. Standard clothing, standard buttons, standard decorations, standard cosmetics, standard housing, standard entertainment, standard foods.

Portland, Maine, to Peshwar. STANDARD.

And there were some slip-ups. The year the Bureau of Research tried to get a grant for the development of space flight they ran into a Coor who was a religious fanatic. A great uncle of Helmut Glass.

"If the Lord wanted us gallivanting all over the universe, he'd have given us wings. We'll put it to the question."

And there was a big row, but the question had spoken of bringing back strange diseases, of calling down the wrath of God.

There it was in the Bu-Opp files. Opinion CG819038331BX: *It is forbidden that man may plan, devise or manufacture any machine intended for transporting humans to any other heavenly body.*

"See the mail rocket, Junior. With about thirty days of work it could take ten men to the moon and back."

"Why don't they do it then?"

"Low-opped."

"Oh."

Standard gravitational attraction of the planet Earth.

Only the people were not standard. In their standard beds they continued to produce humans of odd shapes and sizes and colors. The last stronghold of nonconformity: the standard bed.

Perhaps there was another holdout, too. The language.

High-Opp and Low-Opp were part of the lexicon and all of the derivations thereof. The terms were not always complimentary. A High-Opp could be a person who held a position he didn't deserve. To High-Opp a person could mean to take advantage of him. A Low-

Opp was a person of little worth. To Low-Opp a man could mean to do a man an evil turn or to reduce him in rank. And always in this definition was the implication that the low-opp was by foul means.

Then there were the statuettes. They seemed to appear out of nowhere. Obscene statuettes labeled High-Opp and Low-Opp. Bu-Con was always making raids, uncovering stores of them, sending someone off to the ALP. Still the evil little plastic objects kept appearing.

"Where do they get the materials? Why do they do these things? The State takes care of their needs. (The barren demands of survival.) They have everything they could possibly want. (Their dreams, their Festivals, their two percentum beer, their standard beds. Not to forget the plastic with which to make obscene statuettes.) It's just perversity!"

Let them eat cake!

But she got her head chopped off.

"What do they want now?"

Let them read the ancient books.

"Don't be a fool!"

The scramble in the middle ranks was for privileges, for extra personal possessions, symbols of power. An extra rung on the ladder and what went with it.

Meet Daniel Movius, scrambler. Listen to him.

Low-opped.

Low-opped.

Low-Opped!

Movius pounded his pillow. It was the sense of drabness, eternal drabness. Already he wished for something different. Anything at all, as long as it was different. This was the attraction of the secret Thrill Parlours, the scattered, clandestine schools of the outlawed Separatist Party and their philosophy of Individualism.

Each Man A Separate Individual.

EMASI!

"Individualism in a standardized world? Impossible!"

But the initials blossomed on sidewalks, on walls. *EMASI!* Scrawled inside a stylized side view of a skunk with its tail raised. Stamped in the middle of a sheet of paper which a Com-Burs secretary picked from the fresh stack in the box. Carved on the underside of a toilet seat. And once, just once, painted with an evil-smelling, sticky, tarry substance on The Coor's bedroom walls.

They were still investigating that one.

There were times when the world seemed full of Seps.

Movius wondered if Navvy was a Sep. He turned on his back, stared up at the ceiling. So close. The walls. So close. A cell after his Upper Rank apartment. A brown-walled cell. A Warren.

Was Navvy a Sep? It would make sense. It wasn't difficult to imagine Navvy scrawling EMASI! Somewhere, on a wall. On the seat of the Liaitor's new suit.

Movius sat bolt upright. *Great Roper! Could that have been Navvy?* Slowly, thoughtfully, he eased himself back to the pillow.

The afternoon wore on, a grey progression of bitter thoughts and unanswered questions. Who did this to me? Glass?

He became aware of a new sensation, one he had to think far back in memory to recall. Hunger. He glanced at his wristwatch. Six. Serving time. The bed creaked as he stood up. He felt stiff, as though he'd spent a full hour on the wrestling mat with Okashi.

The Warren dining room was a place of droning conversation, clattering crockery, steaming odors of pallid foods. His tray was shoved back to him with the Standard Thursday Evening Meal. Movius carried the food to an isolated table in the corner. Fried mush, mashed potatoes with synthetic gravy containing vegetable minerals and vitamins. Something that passed for coffee and in a cracked cup. A bowl of pale green jelly substance for dessert.

Movius was aware of the eyes following him, of the unasked questions. The little silences. He picked up his fork. The first bite brought back another memory of his father, the bitter father. "Swill! Make a man's world flat and insipid enough and he won't care if you send him to an early grave!"

In spite of his hunger, Movius had to force himself to eat. He told himself it was the lack of spices to which he had become accustomed in the privileged dining rooms, that the food was the same. He knew it wasn't true. In spite of all the Bu-Blah shouting to the contrary, he knew it wasn't the same food. The Upper Ranks might be eating mashed potatoes and gravy tonight, but there'd be butter in the potatoes, real meat in the gravy. The fried mush might contain chicken and fresh vegetables. The coffee would be real coffee and the dessert would have fresh fruit in it.

Privileges.

How many generations had counted good food a privilege?

He was finishing the mashed potatoes when a man bent over his table. The man exuded a steaming odor of perspiration.

"New here, ain't you?" He touched Movius' lapel.

"What's a Third Ranker doing eating in a Warren Dining Room? Get caught out late?"

They were never as bold as this in the streets. Only among their own, with that solid feeling of approval, of common hate behind them.

"I live here," said Movius.

"Oh?" The man's eyes were two tiny ink dots, bird eyes, unwinking. "What's a Third Ranker doing living in a Warren?"

"I'm back where I started," said Movius.

The man reached out, grasped Movius' lapel, jerked it. "Then get rid of that damn' T, mister. An' put some dye on that fancy color. You ain't no bettern' the rest of us!"

"Leave him alone, Mike."

Movius looked up to his left. The speaker was a giant of a woman in a cook's uniform and carrying a long cleaver. "He just come in today," she said. "Low-opped this morning."

"Keep your nose out of this, Marie Cotton," said the man. "We know he was just low-opped."

She leaned toward him. "You want a little something extra in your mashed potatoes? Some glass, maybe?" She held the cleaver under his chin. "Some of your own gore?"

The man drew back.

The cook stared at him, pressing him back with her eyes until he returned to his seat, face red. She turned to Movius. "Our seamstress is just down the hall from you. She'll do that job on your lapels for some extras from your rations or some loose credits." The woman turned, marched toward the kitchen, suddenly stopped and announced to the room, "We got a peaceful Warren here. We ain't never had no trouble and we ain't gonna have none."

Memory came back to Movius out of his childhood. The cooks ran the Warrens. District Housing appointed managers, of course, but tenants laughed at a manager's orders. A manager was just one step above an LP. *Look at 'im puttin' on airs!* A cook, though—she could make your food bitter, put something in it to make you sick, give you short portions. You didn't cross a cook.

Just one element of the situation bothered Movius. Why had the cook defended him? A fresh low-opp should have been fair game. He took his tray to the wash dump, returned to his room. The question about the book was put out of his mind. It was almost time to follow the instructions given by Navvy's sister. If he was going to follow them. What was her name? Gladys? No. Grace. That was it, Grace. He remembered Navvy talking about her and about their father. The old man had a peculiar first name. Quilliam, Quilliam London. He'd been a professor of some kind once until his classes were low-opped.

Her instructions said he was to go to the Carhouse, see this Clancy. Well, why not? At least it was something different. And Navvy was right this morning. (Damn his secretive manner.)

The dusk flowed with after-dinner noises of children, giggling couples, cat-calls. A man standing across the street watched Movius' retreating back, threw down a cigaret, turned and followed. Soon he picked up a companion. They strolled along, not talking like the other strollers.

Movius turned a corner, saw a long car facing him, dim in the gathering darkness. The car headlights turned on, blinding him and in that instant something sharp bit into his arm. A needle! Unconsciousness swept over his mind. He didn't even feel the hands support him, ease him into the car. Just time for one brief thought: *I should have been more caref . . .*

It was a cell, barren of everything except a hard pallet. Movius opened his eyes, felt the pallet beneath him, absorbed a first awareness of his surroundings. The memory came back slowly—the street, the headlights, the stinging in his arm. He jerked upright, stared around him. The cell was about eight feet long, six wide, eight high. No doors or windows. That was odd. And the walls, a disturbing shade of red. He swung his feet to the floor, rubbed his arm where the needle had punctured it. *Who?*

The answer came almost immediately. An end wall swung back, admitting a pinch-faced man carrying a canvas chair. Movius recognized him immediately: Nathan O'Brien, chief of Bu-Psych. *What does Bu-Psych want with me? And O'Brien?* Movius remembered him as a man who always held something in reserve, never fully committing himself.

O'Brien opened his canvas chair, sat down opposite Movius, calculated, deliberate movements. The dark eyes snapped up at Movius. "Hello, Dan."

What does he expect me to say? Hello, Nate? Movius stared back silently, waiting.

"Sorry if we've inconvenienced you in any way."

"I'll bet you are," said Movius. He decided he had enough hate left over for O'Brien, another part of the system that had degraded him.

"We had to do it that way," said O'Brien. "Two of the Coor's men were following you. No time to explain. They were waiting for a quiet stretch in which to pick you up."

Movius jerked his head around, looked into O'Brien's eyes. "Pick me up? Why would the Coor want me? I thought he was just going to send me off to the ALP."

O'Brien rubbed at a greying temple. "I see you already know. And why is he doing it? Let's say that he likes to demonstrate that he can do away with a person and he doesn't want you running out on his plans. You happen to be a . . . well, an inconvenience. It's a much greater demonstration of power when you use violent methods on a mere inconvenience."

"I don't believe it."

"That's your privilege, Dan."

Movius felt the anger rising in him. He raised his voice. "How could he do it? Can he predict the opp? And if so, how?" He almost shouted the last words.

O'Brien spoke in a quiet, even voice. "The Coor could predict the opp several ways. He and the rest of Com-Burs—myself included—can frame the question to make the answer practically a foregone conclusion. When The Coor wants to be absolutely certain, he sends the question out with a code number held only by a selection of people who know how to answer things his way."

"He can't bypass the Selector," said Movius, his voice more subdued.

"Do you really believe that?" asked O'Brien.

Movius shrugged. What could he believe? As sure as Roper, Glass had made a point of telling him the answer to the question was known before it should have been known.

O'Brien said, "You ought to see my list of district governors, city mayors, managers, their assistants and the families of all of them, who have special numbers manually filed in the Selector. Who ever questions the operator of the Selector when he comes back and says, 'This is the code number?'"

"I suppose the question on my department was sent through on one of those numbers."

O'Brien nodded. "Number 089. In view of the question, it was hardly necessary, but The Coor evidently wanted to be certain."

Movius caught himself taking short, jerky breaths, fought to control his nerves. "How do they keep a secret like that? So many people!"

"There are two answers," said O'Brien. "They don't keep it a secret. I'll wager you've heard it and . . ."

"Yes, but just a rumor."

"What else is a good secret? It's no secret. I know it. Lots of other people know it. You know it. The other answer is that they do keep it a secret. They . . ."

Movius held up his hand. "You just said . . ."

"I know. But it is kept a secret from the main body of the LP. The Seps try to spread the word, but who believes the Seps? Those harebrains! Besides, believing Seps can be dangerous. How are you going to believe something when you don't listen to it in the first place?"

Movius rubbed his eyes with the heels of his hands. How indeed? He said, "I believe it."

"But look what it took to make you believe it," said O'Brien. He sounded exasperated, like a teacher with a dense student. "It's the flaw in their armor, of course. Get a man angry enough, bitter enough, he'll believe almost anything."

Movius said, "But if you keep him from getting angry—keep him apathetic and his stomach filled, he won't even listen. He'll be too tired."

In a pedantic voice, O'Brien said, "Hunger elicits the first anger response of the baby. So, as you say, keep him from being hungry."

"Or convince him he knows everything already," said Movius.

"That, too."

"Why are you telling me all this?" said Movius.

"Oh, yes, our little visit." O'Brien's attitude became more brisk. "Movius, The Coor wanted your fiancée and he needed to demonstrate to . . . uh, others that he has the power of life and death. That is why you were low-opped."

"That's still no answer to my question."

"One moment," said O'Brien. "Today, you saw Glass with your fiancée."

Movius pounded a fist into the palm of his hand. *How did O'Brien know who I saw today?* "You haven't answered my question," Movius repeated.

"Please be patient. As you know, an order will go out tomorrow morning for you to report to the ALP. This is mostly to demonstrate that such . . . uh, accidents can be arranged. And also gets you out of the sight of the lovely Miss Lang. Not that I imagine such drastic measures were needed to gain the same end. There are other reasons."

Now we're getting to it, thought Movius. He said, "Such as?"

"You were a Third Ranker. Were you aware that you were the only man in government above the Fifth Rank who started from the LP? You climbed up there in twelve years. Under this form of government, with so many more places needed for the large families of the . . . uh, High-Opps, that is a dangerous rate of climb. Dangerous to the men it might displace. I believe some of them voiced their fears."

"The same opportunity open to all!" said Movius. Just some more of the old official pap. *Eat your vitalac, little dear, if you want to grow up and be Coordinator. Dangerous rate of climb. Watch out you don't eat too much vitalac, dear. You might become dangerous.* "So they send me off to die in the ALP," he said.

"Mortality rate of seventeen point four," said O'Brien in his precise manner. "With a little pushing in the right place, a promise of reprieve to someone else in the penalty service, the mortality rate becomes one-hundred percentum for one Daniel Movius."

He still hasn't answered my question, thought Movius. *Mr. Bu-Psych wants something from me.* He said, "What do I do now?"

"That depends on several things," said O'Brien. "In about six weeks a second work order will come through. This will be the legal one and it will put you in Bu-Trans."

"Why bother with a work order for a dead man?"

"To cover up the false order. That . . . uh, accidental order would be turned up, somebody in Bu-Labor, somebody inconvenient, would be low-opped."

Movius thought, *If I could hide until that one comes through, wouldn't that be embarrassing to them? Wouldn't it, though?* He said, "Is there a way to hide me?"

"Perhaps."

What does he mean perhaps?

"The second work order is for Bu-Trans," said O'Brien as though he had not already made that point. "Warren Gerard put some special requirements into the sorter today. He's prepared to wait because he half suspects the order can't be filled. He doesn't know that your card already has come out of the sorter, fitting his demands more precisely than he could have expected."

"This doesn't make sense," said Movius. He stood up, looked down on O'Brien.

"Sit down," said O'Brien. "You have to hear me out."

"Oh, I have to hear you out." Movius felt himself breathing too rapidly. He thought, *I've been swallowing everything this little pipsqueak says. How do I know what his game is?*

"Would you prefer the ALP?" asked O'Brien.

"You haven't told me what your game is," said Movius.

"I will, though. Sit down and hear what I have to say. Believe me, it's important."

Movius returned to the pallet. "All right, but shorten it."

"As briefly as possible." O'Brien scratched at the corner of an eye. "Gerard is in a very shaky position at the top of Bu-Trans. His Achilles heel is his Department CR-14, Confidential Routing as it is listed in the table of organization. This department is the government's top secret spying group."

"In Bu-Trans?" Movius' whole face showed his disbelief.

"Who ever looks at a Bu-Trans truck?" asked O'Brien. "It goes about its business and no one notices. For that matter, who ever gives a second glance to the workmen with such a vehicle?"

"What's worrying Gerard?"

"The Coor's nephew, Rafe Newton, is director of CR-14. The Coor and Loren Addington . . ."

"Mr. Police?"

"The same. Only we call him Mr. Bu-Con. These two are set to replace Gerard with Newton."

"What does this mean to me?"

O'Brien acted like a man about to unfold a master-piece. He spread out his hands. "Gerard's requirements are for a man to clean out the vipers in CR-14."

"And I fit this billing?"

"That's right."

"Why are they after Gerard?"

"Next to The Coor, Gerard is the most powerful man in government. At least potentially. He has the biggest organization, larger even than Bu-Con, but not larger than Bu-Con and several of the others upon whom The Coor is depending. It is what was once known as a 'balance of power'. It is a very delicate . . ."

"All right, let's get to the point." Again Movius lifted himself to this feet. "What is it that you want, O'Brien?"

O'Brien looked up at Movius, put a finger to a greying temple, scratched. "You are the direct type, aren't you, Dan? That's good. I want you to spy on the spies . . . for me."

Movius found himself chuckling without humor. "Up here at the top you're just one big happy family."

"You could say that." O'Brien got to his feet. "Do you need time to come to a decision?"

"What choice do I have? If I don't throw in with you, I go to the ALP." Movius shrugged. "Where do I hide?"

"Good Gallup!" said O'Brien. "I'm not going to hide you."

"But you . . ."

"There was a woman waiting for you at the Warren today. She . . ."

"Is she another of your spies?"

"Her? Oh, my, no. She's a Separatist. For precisely

the same reasons which make you valuable to Gerard and myself and dangerous to the government, the Separatists are seeking to enlist your services. They are in a better position to hide you since I will be suspect."

"This woman will hide me?"

"She and her friends."

"Does she have many friends?"

"Grace London? She's a nurse at the district infirmary in the Warren where she lives. Whole building's subversive. Good Seps all."

"I suppose I repay them by spying on them."

"You needn't bother." O'Brien moved toward the wall which had opened to admit him.

"You already had spies in their organization?"

"Let us say that the Seps don't worry me half as much as The Coor." O'Brien spoke without turning. "I presume Miss London gave you instructions on how to meet her?"

"Yes."

The wall swung back ahead of O'Brien. "Then I'll have you dropped off where you may follow those instructions."

You fatuous, self-satisfied low-opp, thought Movius. *Got me right where you want me, haven't you? You and your big head full of intricate thoughts! We'll see, damn you!*

Chapter 4

The Carhouse was a sprawling two-story building pierced by deep, gloomy ramps to the parking levels. Movius noticed the Sep slogan, EMASI! scrawled on a wall where a cleaning crew had missed it. Perhaps on purpose.

Every Man A Separate Individual!

Unless he gets stamped STANDARD first, thought Movius.

At one corner of the building an arrow sign read OFFICE. Movius followed the arrow inside, found one man, a thin, straw-colored figure whose energy ran to quick, short movements of hands and eyes.

"You Movius?"

"Yes."

"Take these." He handed Movius a key and note. "Down that ramp, second door on your left. It's locker eighty." He seemed anxious for Movius to be gone.

Movius said, "Thanks," followed the man's directions.

It was between shifts and the Carhouse was a cavern of echoing footfalls, distant humming of power transmitters. The locker room held a thick odor of perspiration and dust as though in colloidal suspension. It was a long narrow place, steel lockers on both sides, benches down the center. Easy to imagine the room clanging with slammed doors and hurrying men at shift change. The clothes in locker eighty smelled of machine oil, fitted him loosely. Movius ran a hand along the bottom of the locker. As he had expected, it came away greasy. He smeared a streak of the grease along one jaw, spread it around his hands, under his nails. A rag on one of the locker hooks took off some of the grease, leaving enough for effect.

From the pockets of his good suit, Movius transferred the few items he carried — identification, penknife, stylus, notepad. He rolled the good suit into a bundle, tossed it into the locker.

Clancy's note told him to take the employee's elevator to the City Repair Service subway, catch shuttle fifty-one to the Bennington sub-prime generator station. Movius located the elevator in a side hall, descended to the subway, boarded the shuttle. He was relieved to find he was the only passenger. What could he tell a foreman he was doing? The automatic conductor flashed DESTINATION? He punched for Bennington, took a seat by the door. *Now what?* He wondered. This morning the Liaitor would have turned in any Sep he found. *Now I have to ask them to hide me.* The shuttle began to tremble as it gathered speed. Movius leaned back, waited.

Presently, the shuttle began to slow, rocking gently. It stopped, the front light flashing BENNINGTON. Movius stepped out onto the platform, immediately felt the humming presence of the generators through his shoes. A stranger leaned against the wall at one side of the platform. Movius glanced at him, looked away. *I have to act casual,* he thought. He risked another look. *Navvy!* He was wearing off-duty browns, but his complexion was ruddy, cheeks fatter, hair a difficult color.

Movius strode toward him.

Navvy pushed away from the wall. "How did you recognize me?"

"The slouch," said Movius. "I could always tell my car by the look of you slouched against it."

Navvy grinned. "I'll have to work on that. Come on."

"Where?"

"My father's place. Were you followed?"

"Who would want to follow me?"

"The Coor's thuggees."

Movius remembered what O'Brien had said about followers. "There were some earlier, but I don't think they followed me here." He debated telling Navvy about O'Brien, decided to wait, see what the situation was.

"I suspect we'd better do some ducking about," said Navvy. "This way." They went into the service elevator. Navvy took it up, stopped between floors. He did something complicated to the controls with a piece of string, led the way out the escape hatch and into a conduit tunnel so low they had to bend their heads to walk. Movius heard the elevator start up behind them.

That's a trick I'll have to learn, he thought.

Navvy produced a tiny flashlight, picked a way between the maze of pipes. His shadow was a hovering bat on the ceiling. The tunnel smelled of dampness and some chemical, acrid and biting in the nostrils. He couldn't place it. Several times Navvy glanced back to see if Movius was still following.

"Smell the chlorine?" asked Navvy. "They caught eight Seps in here last month. Gassed them all."

Movius felt a trapped sensation, imagined himself caught in here with the rolling clouds of gas pouring down on him. Navvy showed no sign he even considered this possibility. Movius thought of all the times he had sat behind Navvy in the car, never once suspecting him of this sort of knowledge. Never questioned how Navvy got the car to some destination. Never thought of him being a Sep. If Grace was a Sep, as O'Brien had said, then Navvy had to be one, too. And the father, also. Probably a ringleader, that one.

The tunnel branched. They took the left turning. Movius felt his neck beginning to ache from the bent-over walking. It seemed they had come five miles.

"How far have we come?" he whispered.

Navvy spoke over his shoulders in a normal tone. "A little over a mile. There's a turning down here about a quarter of a mile. We take that for about a hundred yards to another elevator."

The elevator well was a faintly-illuminated grey hole, narrow rungs of a ladder going up the wall beside the tunnel mouth. Navvy leaned out, grasped a rung, climbed upward. Movius followed. They came out in a sewer service dome. Navvy fiddled with the lock, opened the door a crack, peered out. "Come on." He ducked through; Movius followed. The door clicked shut behind them.

It was another Warrenate, gloomy under the dim illumination of widely spaced street lights. Movius could distinguish the outline of the Council Hills section above the building on his right. Clouds over the hills held a rosy glow. Lights in the towering apartments had a warm look of elevated privacy. Behind one of those lights up there—Cecelia and Helmut. Or maybe they were one of the dark places. The tired muscles in his fingers reminded him he had been clenching and unclenching his fists.

"This way," said Navvy.

They crossed the street, strolled down the walk, trying to act casual.

"We're to meet a couple of men who'll tell us which route is open," said Navvy. "Lots of Bu-Con patrols out tonight."

Three men came out from between buildings on their left, approached, walking abreast. When they were about ten feet away, Movius recognized the one on the right. The Coor's bodyguard from the hallway outside Cecelia's apartment. Something glinted in the man's hand. Instinctively, Movius ducked, crying out a warning to Navvy. He dove toward the man, heard the sharp *fap!* of a gun over his head. The men went down before him. Movius got the gun hand, brought the edge of his other hand down hard above the bridge of the man's nose, remembering all the times in the gym when Okashi had cautioned him to use this blow lightly. It could kill a man. The gunman went limp.

Movius rolled over, avoiding the full force of a kick aimed at his head by another of the men. It caught him on the jaw and he tasted blood. Movius rolled away, hooked a toe behind the kicker's ankle, slammed his other foot into the man's knee. There was a crack of broken bones. The man screamed and toppled over backwards. Movius charged to his feet, kicked a hand away from a gun pocket, brought the foot down on the man's face. He whirled, saw Navvy rolling on the sidewalk with the third one. Movius grabbed up the fap-gun which had fallen from the body guard's hand, waited until Navvy's opponent rolled uppermost, and cracked the man on the head with the gun. Navvy stood up, feeling gingerly of his neck.

A car turned at the end of the street.

"Let's get out of here!" Navvy took Movius' arm, led the way running between the buildings and around the rear. As they turned the corner, Movius glanced back, saw the car stop beside the fallen attackers, disgorge four men. One man he recognized—Loren Addington, the fat chief of Bu-Con. Movius felt the gun in his hand, all of the hate seeming to flow out through that hand. Here was one of the Com-Burs High-Opps who had put him in this position. He lifted the gun, fired twice at the figures beside the car, saw one topple, clutching his side. Not Addington, though; the fat man ducked behind his car.

Movius felt Navvy tugging at his arm. "Come on!"

They found an open service entrance to a Warren, ran down a flight of steps to a boiler room, behind the boiler to the conduit tunnel. "Thank Roper for standard construction," panted Navvy. "We're somewhere under Richmond Warrenate. Have to get out of here before they block off the tunnels, smoke us out. We'll head northeast."

It seemed they were an hour running in the tunnels, down ladders, up ladders, twisting, turning. Movius was hopelessly turning around. For some reason, he didn't think about that. He was remembering the fight. He couldn't explain to himself why the action had left him feeling refreshed. It was as though he had needed the violence. The battle had been like a catharsis, easing the tensions inside him. He felt washed clean, ignored the pain in his jaw where the man had kicked him.

Navvy slowed and Movius began to consider the implications of the fight. He called out softly, "How did they know where to find us?"

Navvy stopped, wiped perspiration from his forehead. "I've been thinking about that, too. I think someone spotted you talking to Clancy."

"Oh?"

"And they made Clancy talk."

"How much did Clancy know?"

"Only that I was going to meet my friends near that sewer service dome."

"Fine friends!"

"They may have been picked up."

"And Clancy didn't know anything else?"

Navvy shook his head. "Not even where we meet. He's new."

"What will they do to Clancy?"

"A body in the river. He knew the chance he took."

Movius thought about Clancy, quick-moving, alive. Now a dead thing in the river. *So that's the kind of a fight it is? But I knew that.* In a subdued tone, he said, "Let's go."

They stayed in the tunnels, first on one level, then another. Twice they smelled the residue of chlorine. The tunnel opened finally into another boiler room, from there into a smaller storage room occupied by five people, four men and a woman. The room pulsed with a faint vibration which made him uneasy, his skin tingly. Then he recognized it—he was near an unmounted scrambler, a portable one. No spy beam could penetrate this room. It wouldn't even react to the room. No room. He was almost close enough to touch the people before he recognized the woman as the mouse-creature who had directed him here—Grace London. Strange that he had remembered her as sallow, grey. Her face held a clean, lively look now. And her hair was out of the bun, rolling back softly from her forehead. She wasn't beautiful, but she had something. He decided the word was vitality.

An old man stood beside her. That would be Navvy's father, Quilliam London. The old man snorted. "You gave us a scare."

"What happened to our escort?" asked Navvy.

"I sent Bowden and Ladde," said Quilliam London. "They were picked up by a patrol. That stupid Bowden had a grease pencil in his pocket with some grit from a concrete wall still in it. They knew what he'd been writing on the walls."

Navvy paled. "Did they take them in for . . ."

"They tried to fight their way out of it," said Quilliam London. "Now we need two more couriers." He turned to Movius. "Good to see you, Mr. Movius. Won't you sit down?"

Come into my parlour, thought Movius. He had an instant feeling of dislike for the old man. Too cold about those poor couriers.

Quilliam London motioned for Navvy to pull out folding chairs from a corner of the storage room. A flickering orange glow from the open door of the boiler room washed over the old man's face as he turned. It gave him a hawk-like, demoniacal look. The others in the room moved closer and Movius saw that one of those he had thought to be a man actually was another woman, a flat-chested giant. . . . Eyes widening, he recognized her. The cook. Marie something, from the Warren. The one who had silenced the LP tough. Movius nodded to her.

"Sit down," said Quilliam London. Movius took one of the chairs. The old man bent his stiff frame into a chair opposite and scratched at his chin. "My son here is a very discerning young man, Mr. Movius. He feels you would be valuable to our cause. For that reason, I've gathered here some people whose information you will find interesting. First, Mr. Janus Peterson." London sounded vaguely like the announcer at the festival shows.

A beefy, muscular man on Movius' right hitched a chair forward. As the man moved closer, Movius saw that he was built like a barrel, with really tremendous girth. Janus Peterson. He had large, wide-set blue eyes which blinked rapidly before he spoke. A flat nose gave him the look of a fighter.

Peterson's eyes blinked like shutters. "Mr. Movius, my brother-in-law works in Bu-Labor." The voice was husky. "He's a kind of a clerk. He give me this today." The man extended a piece of paper. Movius took the paper, glanced at it, looked back to Peterson. The man said, "That's a carbon of an order sent out to Bu-Supply today. It says to get an issue of Arctic clothing ready for a Daniel Movius who is going into the ALP. That's your number, ain't it?"

Movius looked at the number. Yes, it was his. He nodded. So this was the LP grapevine. Efficient. He gave Navvy a searching look. Navvy winked at him.

Quilliam London grasped the arm of a man at his right, leaned forward. "This is Arthur VanDyne. He's in Bu-Labor." Again that vague suggestion of a man announcing the next act. Something a little off-beat here.

Arthur VanDyne was a pale-faced, frightened-looking little man who sat on the edge of his chair, knees close together. "I'm a file clerk, Mr. Movius," he said. The man's voice was high-pitched, squeaky. "Sometimes when I'm working in the files I hear things. They're high, the files, you understand, and if someone is on the other side of the files, in the other aisle, talking, you can hear them quite well if you put your ear to the metal."

Movius had a mental picture of Arthur VanDyne with his pale, frightened face bent close to a filing case, listening. It was a disquieting picture, somehow. He wondered how many there were like this. Frightened. Listening.

VanDyne cleared his throat in a precise manner, found a handkerchief and dabbed at his lips. "I heard two of the confidential clerks talking today." He replaced the handkerchief in a pocket, clasped his hands in his lap. "They're the ones who work directly out of the chief's office. One said, 'We got this order out of the Sorter today, but the chief said to lose it for about six weeks. Why do you suppose he wants us to do that?' And the other one said, 'Don't ask too many questions. What's the guy's name?' Then the first one said, 'Daniel Movius, number . . .'" He fumbled in a pocket. "Here, I wrote it down."

Movius took the paper. It was his number.

VanDyne went on: "Then the second one asked, 'Where's he going?' And the first one said, 'CR-14 in Bu-Trans, whatever that is.' And that's all I know, Mr. Movius."

"We've already met, haven't we, Mr. Movius?" It was the big cook, still with that casual look of authority the cooks had.

Movius nodded, wondering what connection she had with this business. One thing sure—she'd saved him from a nasty time back there in the Warren dining room.

"My sister is in Bu-Trans," said the woman. "Her name is Tyle Cotton and she works in the armory, passing out weapons. She used to be . . ." The woman paused, wet her lips with her tongue.

"She used to run his bedroom," the cook said. "That was before she got blocky like me. Gerard's a big-headed little squirt, bald as an egg, really little, but he likes his women large. The bigger the better, but curvy, not square." Again the cook wet her lips with her tongue. "My sister hates Gerard; and she's been working with the head of CR-14, Rafe Newton, to get Gerard."

"Oh?" That agreed with what O'Brien had said.

"CR-14 is the spy outfit for the government," said the woman. "It's really important. It used to be Gerard's ace in the hole; now he's losing it."

"What's this have to do with me?" asked Movius.

Quilliam London extended a long, bony finger, tapped Movius on the knee. "Gerard fed some job specifications into the Sorter today. He doesn't know yet, as Arthur here pointed out, that your card came up fitting those specifications. He will know it, though, given time."

"About six weeks?" asked Movius.

London nodded, scratched his chin. "If you report for work, Gerard is going to give you the job of cleaning out this Department CR-14."

"Just like that?"

"You fit his specifications." London narrowed his eyes almost to slits. "You know what we are, of course?"

"You're Seps."

"That's right. Can you imagine how valuable it would be to us to have a man in the government's spy organization?"

"I have a rough idea." Movius glanced at Navvy standing behind his father. "Can you hide me?"

Quilliam London said, "I believe so."

"There's one thing still not clear to me," said Movius. "Why did Glass do this to me?"

The old man stood up, unbending slowly. He looked like a knobby walking stick. "Mr. Glass wanted your fiancée. We have found that Mr. Glass usually gets what he wants and keeps it until he is tired of it."

That was what O'Brien had said. *It must be true then.* Movius felt more confidence in the LP grapevine than he had in O'Brien. *Helmut Glass! You want somebody's woman? You just flick a little finger and that somebody falls over dead. Not yet, Helmut!*

"What kind of an organization do you have?" asked Movius.

London put his thick-veined hands on his knees. "We don't have anything worthy of the name."

"But the Separatist . . ."

"A great many disjointed, bitter people from Cairo to Kalamazoo, but without any binding force."

Movius let a glance flick over the people around him. "What do you do?"

"These are my students," said Quilliam London. "I have a class in semantics. I teach people how to avoid the controlling influences of others. It's largely a matter of discovering what the other person actually wants."

"Why do you do it?"

A kind of fire came into London's eyes, like the moving orange light from the boiler room behind him. The other people in the room stirred restlessly. Grace London coughed.

"I'm going to beat them," said the old man. "Now we're a herd following the whim of their loaded questions. When we start seeing through their questions to the things they secretly want, their days are numbered."

"And I can help in this?"

London permitted a slight touch of scorn to creep into his voice. "That should be obvious from the trouble we've taken on your behalf."

"How do I fit into this?"

"You're an expert at influencing people," said London.

It was not the answer Movius had expected. "Me?"

"Yes. The Liaitor. You smoothed the way between differing groups. You influenced people who were themselves experts at influencing people. You made people see things your way, somewhere between their two opposed stands. You influenced them."

"I'd never thought of it that way."

London's eyes widened. "Then how did you operate?"

"I'd just sit down and listen to what the people had to say and, somehow, a compromise they'd accept always occurred to me."

"I see." The way Quilliam London said it made it plain he didn't see, but that he would let it go. "What do you know about Bu-Psych?"

Did he imagine it or did the room suddenly become tense. Maybe they had seen O'Brien's driver let him out. Perhaps this was the point to tell them about the visit with O'Brien. Yes, this was the place. He told them.

"And he knew I'd seen you in the Warren?" asked Grace London, her voice flat.

Movius looked at her. She didn't seem surprised. "That's right."

Quilliam London's voice broke in, too eager. "We've a spy of our own to find." He looked around at Navvy. "Get on that right away, Navvy."

"Yes." Navvy didn't look at his father.

"Perhaps some planted information," said Movius. "Trace it out the other end."

"What I had in mind," said London.

They didn't seem very concerned, thought Movius. *It's no wonder they've never made any progress. All theory and no action. They need someone to pull things together. With some good organization, O'Brien would never be able to get a line on them.*

He said, "And you've no master coordination at all?" Still it seemed almost unbelievable.

"None."

Again Movius thought they became tense.

Quilliam London said, "The Separatist movement is contained in the massive unrest of the populace. There are other schools such as mine. I've heard rumors. Auckland, Berlin, Paris . . . But it is well for one person not to know too much. Bu-Con has sharp eyes and large ears."

This could be pulled together into a tight organization, thought Movius. He stood up, went to the door of the boiler room, turned. "Navvy." How different the name sounded here than in the car.

"Yes, sir." Still the *air*.

"Could your friends smuggle my things out of the other Warren?"

"Is it necessary?"

Was it necessary? Movius clenched, unclenched his fists. "I've personal papers, reports, notes and other things I'll be needing."

"Right." Another silence. Navvy pulled at his lower lip. "Needing for what?"

Movius ignored the question, returned to his chair. "How could I have remained so blind."

"Protective coloration," said London.

"What?"

"In a world where seeing too much is dangerous,

blindness is a virtue."

In that moment, the old man reminded Movius of his own father. Too bad they'd never met. Movius stood up, pounding a fist into the palm of his hand. No coordination. No organization. Nothing with which to strike back. He felt angry with these people. So much they could have done and they'd done absolutely nothing. "Why don't you have an organization?"

"We've never had anyone with the drive and ability to lead us," said Quilliam London.

Again that tense stillness in the room.

No one to lead them. It was as though they were asking him to take over. Movius returned to the boiler room door, looked at the dancing flame. *I'd have to play it delicately, more delicately than anything I met as Liaitor.* In the orange flame he seemed to see an image of Helmut Glass. It brought a quick knotting of hate. Movius turned slowly, strode back to Quilliam London. "All right, London." His voice had the old commanding power of the Liaitor, but with overtones of violence he'd never suspected were in him. "I've just put the question, cast the opp and polled myself into your job."

The old man nodded. "Good."

"Under my own conditions," said Movius.

"Yes?" The hunter's eyes seemed to be watching him, ready to pounce.

"We'll run things my way. No organization! I'm going to organize. No coordination! I'm going to coordinate. I'm the new Sep coordinator. And maybe . . ."

Quilliam London leaned toward him. "Maybe what?"

"Nothing. We're going to blast those High-Opps right out of their seats!"

"That's what we had in mind," said London.

"You accept?" He had expected an argument.

The old man's smile was reserved. "You leave us no choice."

Movius looked away, turned back to Navvy. "Where are you going to hide me?"

Navvy looked down at his father.

"Best get him settled," said Quilliam London.

"Right away, father." To Movius, "This way, sir."

Still that damned *sir*, thought Movius.

It was a hidden room a few feet into the tunnel. They had to squirm over the tops of pipes, wriggle sideways through an opening hardly more than a crack. Navvy dropped a black curtain, clicked a switch. A single light illuminated an oblong cell about fourteen feet by eight. The shadow of an alcove was a black square at the opposite end of the room.

"We tapped the conduits for power," said Navvy. "There's a washroom of sorts in the alcove down there." He held back the entrance curtain. "See you tomorrow." Before Movius could protest, he was gone.

There was a canvas cot with two blankets. Movius turned off the light, undressed in the dark, put the stolen gun atop his clothes and placed the pile of them beside the cot. The blankets were rough against his skin, not like the smooth sheets of his apartment. *His* apartment!

Low-opped!

There still were so many unanswered questions. Well, tomorrow. He put a hand to his jaw where the man had kicked him. With a fierce vindictiveness, he hoped he'd hit the gunman too hard above the bridge of the nose. Okashi had said it would kill a man.

Something had gone out of him about the time of the flight. The last of the numbness had been replaced by an electric tension. Active hate. Not the *standard* brand at all.

I'm going to get your job, Glass! From now on things are going to be run for Daniel Movius!

He let his hand drop to the floor beside the cot, felt the outline of the gun he had taken from the fallen thuggee. It gave him a sense of power and recalled something he'd read in one of his father's books.

"To make a revolution one must have monstrous inequality, suppression of freedom until the people think of little else. Then there must be someone with that vital spark needed to unify a movement. With that person there must be a belief that nothing is of importance except his cause."

Nothing else of importance.

He fell asleep on the thought, hand touching the gun.

Chapter 5

Helmut Glass — The Coor — reclined on a couch in his apartment, one hand touching a frosted drink on the floor beside him. An atmosphere of Romanesque indolence hovered about him. Part of it was the way he spoke to the two men standing about ten feet from the couch; spoke to them, but never looked at them while he spoke.

"So you missed him." It was a statement, not a question.

One of the standing men stirred. "He walked around the corner from the Warren and when we got there this car was just pulling away. We couldn't catch the number of it. Something was over the number."

"And you didn't recognize the people in the car?" The Coor lifted his head, took a sip of his drink, still not looking at the two men.

"Couldn't even see them."

Glass replaced his drink on the floor, wiped his lips with the back of his hand. "What happened when he came to the Warren?"

The man who had been speaking, looked to his companion, back to The Coor. "He met a woman."

"He what?" Now Glass looked at his men. He sat up. "And what did he and the woman do?"

"They made love," said the man. "We had a peeper

on the apartment, a little portable job, so we couldn't make out their whispering, but they got on the bed and . . ."

"Spare me the details," said Glass. "Did you have the woman followed or is that too much to hope for?"

"Ourran trailed her, but he lost her in the Lascadou District. He said he thinks she ducked into the tunnels."

"That's Ourran's excuse for inefficiency," said Glass. "Did you recognize the woman?"

"She looked familiar, but I couldn't place her." The man looked at the floor.

"And I presume you had no camera to get a picture of her?"

"It wasn't that kind of assignment."

Glass showed signs of restlessness, chewed at his lip. The nervous tic rippled across his cheek. "A badly bungled job. All I asked you to do was to pick him up, hold him overnight and send him off to the ALP in the morning. It seems you can't do a simple little job like that." He drained his drink.

The men shuffled their feet. "I think he has friends in the High-Opp," said the one who had been doing the talking.

The Coor rattled the ice in his glass. "Yes, that's a possible explanation." He looked toward his bedroom where someone could be heard stirring about. "Put a watch on the Warrens. Get Addington to send out search squads."

"We'll keep an eye on the transports, too, sir."

"Do that." Glass suddenly glared up at the man who had been speaking. "And listen to me, Pescado! No more bungling!"

The man lowered his eyes. "Yes, sir. What'll we do with Movius when we find him?"

Glass lifted himself to his feet, again looked toward the bedroom. "Kill him."

"You don't want us to question . . ."

"Good night," said The Coor. "I have some business which requires my attention."

"Kill him it is, sir."

Glass escorted them to the door, returned, mixed two drinks at a portable bar, took them into the bedroom.

Chapter 6

Nathan O'Brien, his back to the night-filled window, stared at Quilliam London for a moment. The old man had just entered the top floor office in the Bu-Psych Building. "Well?"

London took his time sitting down, settled back in the chair, suddenly looked up at O'Brien with those sharp hunter's eyes. "He's the one, all right."

O'Brien relaxed. "I take it you approve?"

"I didn't say that."

"Oh?"

Silence fell between them. London turned, stared at a chart on the wall. It was the chart which had been on the table. The single red line had been moved perhaps a quarter of an inch farther along its mysterious crossing.

"The loyalty index thing?" asked O'Brien.

London nodded. "He moves too quickly. Snap decisions. He made some *fool* statement about not thinking out things. The right solution always comes to him. I'm afraid he may turn ruthless."

"That makes a good revolutionary."

"Depends on the revolution."

O'Brien looked at the red line on the chart. "Do you think he's dangerous?"

"I know he's dangerous." London leaned forward, tapped a yellowed fingernail against the table top.

"Give him a taste of the power that goes with an absolute commander and he'll be dangerous to anyone or anything that crosses him."

"No one is proof against a bullet," said O'Brien.

"That is exactly what I mean," said London. "You and I are mortal."

O'Brien's eyes widened.

"One way thinking is dangerous," said London. "If Movius found out any of the basic elements of our plans—say he discovered that Cecelia Lang deliberately vamped The Coor to get Movius low-opped . . ." He clicked his tongue against the roof of his mouth, a sound surprisingly like that of a fap-gun.

"Who'd do his dirty work?"

"Movius is the kind to do his own dirty work."

"The things which make him ideal for our purposes also make him extremely dangerous to us," said O'Brien. He rubbed a greying temple, sat down across from London. "I guess we anticipated that. Nothing to do but look sharp and do away with him once he's served his purpose."

"Afraid so," said London. "We wouldn't dare let him assume control of the government. I'll alert the others. Any one of us may be called upon to put him out of the way."

"It would be criminal to see our groundwork wasted," said O'Brien. "I presume Grace got across to him the great mystery of it all."

London leaned back in his chair, tipped his head down. "I'm not certain that was such a good idea. Grace was followed, had to lead them clear out of Lascadou before she could shake them."

"Movius does have the idea he's an important figure, though?" asked O'Brien.

"As far as I can see, he has always had that idea."

O'Brien shook his head. "The reports would indicate that he has not been extremely ego-conscious. This business of leading him through the tunnels, mysterious organization, the sudden attention, all of these things are designed to . . ."

"That's another thing," said London. "Navvy and Movius almost got knocked off on the way in tonight. Someone spotted Movius with Clancy and they blanketed the Richmond and Riverside Warrenates. They tortured the information out of Clancy, but he didn't know much."

"What happened?" asked O'Brien.

"Three of The Coor's hoods picked them up coming out of a sewer service dome. Navvy said Movius is an unexpectedly deadly man in a fight or they'd have been done for. Navvy could hardly get Movius away. He stopped and took a shot at Addington."

"Addington? What was he doing . . ."

"After they picked up Clancy, Addington came down to supervise the . . . uh, interrogation himself. Clancy only knew Navvy and Movius were meeting two of our men near that service dome."

"I presume they dropped Clancy in the river?"

"Yes."

O'Brien pulled a stylus from his pocket, scratched the palm of his hand with it. "We're pretty ruthless and callous ourselves, Quilliam."

"In a good cause."

"And we are the judges of how much worth our cause has," said O'Brien. He put the stylus back in his pocket, looked up at the other chart on the wall, his eyes traveling down over the multi-colored lines. "We're going to have a bad time. Crisis is near. Maybe two months, maybe less."

"About the time of The Coor's Fall poll," said London.

"Anything else on your mind, Quilliam? It's been a long day."

London rested his bony elbows on the table. "Guarding Movius when he goes out to answer the Bu-Trans work order."

"I've been thinking about that, too," said O'Brien. "The Bu-Trans starting clerk is a man named Bailey. He has a sister who . . ."

Chapter 7

Movius awoke with the sure knowledge that someone was coming along the tunnel, a slow rustle of
movement. The luminous dial on his watch showed
five minutes to seven. He scooped up the gun from the
floor beside his cot, slipped from the cot, tip-toed to the
light switch, waited. He heard the curtain open, clicked
the switch. The wide, staring eyes of Janus Peterson, the
Bu-Trans driver he had met the night before, stared
back at him. The big man's barrel-shaped body just fitted through the narrow doorway.

"Ready for business, ain't you?" said Peterson,
looking at the gun. The man's eyes began their rapid
blinking. "Sure are ready." In Peterson's husky voice it
was a flat statement, much as a man might say "Not
today."

Movius returned to the cot, tossed the gun onto it
while he dressed. "Sorry. I couldn't know who it was. I
just woke up."

Peterson and another man began bringing in boxes.
"Your stuff," said Peterson. "Had to cart it out through
the garbage disposal tube." He placed a box on the
floor. "Great Gallup! What a stench!" His glance went
to the gun on the cot. "Guy you took that off of died.
Two more of The Coor's boys in the hospital, a Bu-Con
bull's there, too, with a hole in his side." He grinned at

Movius, the action giving his face a mask-like appearance. "Must've been some night!"

The LP grapevine, thought Movius. He said, "Do they know who did it?"

"They didn't recognize who was with you, but they must've spotted you. They're hopping mad and looking all over for you."

"What's the order?"

"I hear it's shoot on sight," said Peterson.

That does it, thought Movius. *If it's a war they want, they'll get one. Damn them!* He said, "We're going to need recruits, Mr. Peterson. Know of any?"

"Might; might not."

That's logical, thought Movius. *How does he know he can trust me?*

"You could try remembering when the time comes," said Movius.

"Might; might not."

Movius smiled. "Thanks."

"I figure you're welcome." Peterson turned, slipped out.

A good man, thought Movius. *He's going to come in handy.*

Quilliam London brought Movius his breakfast. The old man lowered himself to a box, scratched his chin with a thumb. "They're already looking for you."

Movius took his plate, sat on the cot. "Bu-Con?"

"No. Some organization we don't recognize. Nobody knows who the men are."

Movius thought about the efficiency of the LP grapevine, put the plate aside. "Nobody?"

London nodded. "We think it's some special squad The Coor has imported. They're not hunting for you by name. They're just around asking if anyone answering your description has been seen. Some of them have pictures."

"Has my order to the ALP gone out?"

"On the morning round-up. It'll be in the District Circulars by tonight."

"If The Coor's special squad . . ."

"You're worried about answering the Bu-Trans order if and when it comes out." London narrowed his eyes. "If you were married right away . . ."

Movius had picked up his plate, started to resume eating. He looked up sharply. "How's that?"

"You come out of hiding with a wife."

"What good would that do me?"

London bent forward, stood up slowly, stiffly. "You could claim your nuptial off-time. If they dared bring up the ALP thing, you could say you weren't very attentive right after being married. The worst Bu-Con magistrate in the city wouldn't dare say anything after that, especially with you reporting for legal orders."

"I'm not worried about the magistrates."

"There's another aspect to it: Glass might pass you by if you were married—out of the running, so to speak."

"Even after I killed one of his bully boys, maimed two others and shot a Bu-Con operative?" Movius put his plate on a box, got to his feet.

London looked toward the door. "They can't prove it was you." He turned back. "We'll fix you up with an alibi."

Movius shook his head. "It's no good. If The Coor wants me badly enough, he'll go on trying until he gets me . . . or until I get him."

"Glass isn't the only big man in the government," said London.

"Are you referring to that pipsqueak O'Brien?"

London put a hand over his mouth, removed it. "No, I was referring to Warren Gerard."

"That CR-14 thing?"

"Yes. Glass is afraid of Gerard. If you can get Gerard to back you, The Coor may call off his dogs."

Movius looked skeptical. "He may not, too."

"That's the chance we take."

The blood flushed into Movius' face. "You mean that's the chance *I* take!"

"Of course, of course," said London. "But Gerard *does* have a big organization."

"Why would he want to protect me?"

"He needs you."

Movius' voice showed scorn. "Like he needs an extra car and driver."

London ignored the bitter tone. "The Coor and Gerard are about ready for a showdown on the CR-14 issue and The Coor holds the edge right now. Gerard needs help."

"And you think I fit Gerard's requirements?"

"I know you do. I've seen your Sorter card. There's a deviation of .00001 from the requirements and they were tough." London pursed his lips. "High loyalty index, resourcefulness, adaptability, knowledge of the government, no attachments to anyone high in the government . . ."

"Why couldn't I stay in hiding, organize from here?" Movius walked to the corner of the room and back. "That seems the most logical . . ."

"It's not." London faced him from the doorway. "If Glass succeeds in taking over Bu-Trans, he'll have the strength to capture every other department of the government. Our enemy will no longer be divided and they will crack down on the Seps all over the world."

"So I have to save Gerard's neck to save our necks, is that it?"

"That's it. We need a divided government. We need the time to gain strength."

"Even so . . ."

"This is the way things are," said London.

"I meant about the wife," said Movius. "Is that necessary?"

"I believe so. You have to present a good front to Gerard."

Movius shrugged. "Well, where do I find a wife?"

"We thought you might have some woman friend."

Movius thought of his friends. A pack of averted faces! All except Phil Henry. He shook his head. "I know one man I think I could trust. The only woman friend I had is probably sleeping with The Coor right now." He clenched his fists, thrust them into his pockets.

"Miss Lang?"

Movius stared at the wall. "Yes."

"No others?"

"None I could trust."

They were silent while Movius clenched and unclenched his fists until the muscles pained him. "Maybe there's someone in your classes," he said. "It doesn't have to be a real marriage."

"It has to be convincing, though," said London. He lifted the curtain at the doorway, dropped it. "I'll see what I can do."

"We've another problem," said Movius. "You know what Glass will do first. He'll have my number called on the next minor opp. When I go out to register, his men will bottle off the area and comb it. If I don't go out, they sentence me to penalty service the minute I show my face."

"We thought of that," said London. "One of the things we do this morning is make a rubber stamp of your thumbprint. Somebody we trust will report you in miles from here. We'll scatter your registrations until they think you have wings."

Movius paced across the room and back. "That should work." He stopped, looked up at London. "I want to start organizing. We should put out an appeal for recruits, get cell meetings."

London pointed to a stack of boxes against the back wall of the room. "There's a duplicator in there somewhere. Grace knows how to operate it. You start drafting the appeal. I'll send Grace down with our skunk and EMASI! plate."

"Every Man A Separate Individual," said Movius.

"You'll make a good Separatist yet," said London.

Movius shook his head. "You have it wrong. I'm already a Sep. I'll do the making of Seps. Send Grace along."

London's eyes held an odd, speculative light. "I wonder if we made the right choice?" he said.

"Choice of what?"

"Nothing," said London. "I was thinking out loud."

Chapter 8

O'Brien stared at the pigeons on the ledge, wishing they'd stop their senseless cooing and take off to wherever it was they went in the afternoons. Without turning, he said, "What's he doing now?" He turned. "He's had a week to get things moving."

Quilliam London turned away from the multi-colored wall chart. "He's back in his room with Janus Peterson and about a dozen others. He's appointing cell chiefs. He's named Janus . . ."

"Cells?" O'Brien glanced sharply at London. "I had no idea Movius read history."

"His father taught it before it was low-opped."

"Oh, yes. Slipped my mind for a moment. Of course he'd know history. I'm letting myself get too nervous. Must quiet down." O'Brien tugged at his ear.

"He and Grace have put together a strong appeal for recruits," said London. "It's really a masterpiece. It picks up and magnifies every one of the little things you hear the LP's griping about."

O'Brien took his chair at the end of the table, sat down. "What about the marriage?"

London rubbed a finger against his cheek. "Grace is willing. She'll be along in a . . ."

The door opened; Grace slipped in, sank into a chair beside her father. "He's a slave driver," she said. "But he certainly knows how to get things going." She was breathing rapidly as though she had been running.

"We were just talking about the marriage idea," said O'Brien. "It'd be a good thing to have a trusted operative such as yourself near him all the time. And a platonic alliance such as this wouldn't . . ."

Grace stood up, went to the window and appeared to be watching the pigeons. She said, "I think . . ." broke off and put a hand to the glass in front of her.

"Not backing out are you?" asked O'Brien.

She turned, looked from O'Brien to her father. "Father, I . . ."

London frowned. "Are you maybe getting to like him a little too much?"

"Of course not!" She turned back to the window.

"I was just asking," said London. "After all, you have been seeing a great deal of him these past few days and the man is charming."

"It's just so cold-blooded," said Grace, addressing the window.

O'Brien gave his ear a particularly sharp tug. "Revolution is always cold-blooded."

"I suppose so." She looked at her hands, rubbed a finger against the glass. "Well, if we're going to do it, let's get it over with." She turned, looked at O'Brien. "Can you get the marriage registry in so it won't be found until we need it?"

"All taken care of," said O'Brien.

"Maybe we'd better get someone else," said London.

Grace shook her head. "No. Nathan is right. I'm the obvious one for the job."

"But . . ."

"No *buts*, Father. It was your idea, remember?"

"I was afraid you'd remind me of that."

Chapter 9

It was altogether unlike what Movius had imagined his wedding ceremony would be. Navvy came for him at a quarter past seven in the cell-like room off the tunnel.

"Pastor Dillon had to wait until after his regular rounds before he could come," said Navvy. He sat down on the cot, slapped his knee.

Movius almost told him to call it off. He felt a sudden weariness, realized he'd been working steadily since five that morning. So damned much to do, so many people to see and screen. Those tri-di recordings to make and ship off overseas and to the rest of the country.

"You ready?" asked Navvy. He looked up at Movius, an impersonal, scanning look that made Movius uncomfortable.

"Just a minute." He went back to the washroom, washed ink stains off his hands. Again he wondered if it wouldn't be simpler to smuggle him onto one of the skytrains. Personal appearances at the new organizations were much more effective. People liked to see a man before accepting him as a leader. The tri-di recordings were good, though, especially when magnified. Movius dried his hands, returned to Navvy.

"Let's go," said Navvy. He lifted himself to his feet.

Movius sought in his mind for something else to use as a delay. Nothing. "May as well," he said.

In the boiler room the flickering orange light gave an evil cast to the walls. It was almost unbearably hot in the room. Movius felt the perspiration start under his arms, knew he would be sticky and uncomfortable before this was finished.

Pastor Dillon was a frail-bodied man with an angular head, glazed, remote eyes, sing-song voice. "And this is the bride/groom," he said. He held a worn black book opened in his hands. The Bible. Another history book. They'd low-opp that, too, if they dared.

Grace and her father were arguing in whispers. Movius heard her say, "It's only a temporary . . ." She broke off as she saw Movius.

"I understand how things are sometimes," said Pastor Dillon, who also had overheard her. "If you'd like, I could pre-date the license and ceremony, make it appear that the little one was . . ."

"Not necessary!" snapped Quilliam London. He glared at the pastor, patted Grace's shoulder. "As you will, my dear."

Again Movius had the impulse to back out, get another woman for the role. He kept wanting to say something all the while Pastor Dillon intoned the ancient ceremony, but he couldn't find his voice except to respond as directed.

"God bless you and this holy union," said Pastor Dillon in his strange sing-song. "May He watch over you and ever keep you in His holy grace . . . Amen."

Grace, thought Movius. *Holy Grace.* He felt a decidedly unholy impulse to comment on this, but the impulse was stifled when he turned and saw two tears running down her cheeks.

"Kiss her," said Pastor Dillon.

"Wha . . . what?"

"Kiss her. It's customary."

London nodded for him. The hunter eyes had lost some of their directness. Stiffly, Movius took Grace in his arms, kissed her lips, surprised at the salt taste of tears. It was unlike any other kiss of his experience—tremulous, haunting.

Pastor Dillon gave a final blessing, turned, labored up the stairs at the end of the boiler room. They heard a door open, close.

"Well," said Movius.

London took his daughter's arm. "Good night."

Grace did not look at him.

Father and daughter followed the route taken by the pastor, leaving Navvy and Movius in the baleful orange light of the boiler room. It had never more reminded him of the Biblical hell. *Low-opp that, too!* he thought.

Movius found himself unaccountably angry with Navvy. He said, "I can find my way back alone. Go on with them!"

Navvy looked at him, shrugged, went up the stairs.

The hidden room was a dank, cold place after the boiler room. Movius turned off the light, threw himself onto the cot. The memory of Grace's low voice answering Pastor Dillon, the frightened look on her face, the tears, the tremulous kiss, all kept intruding on his other thoughts. He sat up, undressed in the dark, crawled between the blankets, feeling somehow cheated.

In the days that followed, Movius found himself often brought up sharp as he looked at Grace. *That's my wife! Great Gallup!*

And Grace, when she saw him looking at her this

way, blushed, went more quickly about her work.

There wasn't much time for personal thoughts, though. More cells were being organized, more recorded speeches made. The local organization passed the sixteen thousand mark.

In one month, nine of Movius' couriers were caught, but they destroyed their packages with their incendiaries, killed themselves with a quick poison in a false tooth.

Chapter 10

Helmut Glass, his square face set in an angry frown, paced his office atop the Com-Burs Building. It was a sybarite's office—soft carpets, chairs with deep cushions, a bar in the corner, dark paneling. An aroma of some wood perfume mingled in the air with the smoky residue of rare tobacco.

Across from Glass, on a coffee-brown leather couch, sat Loren Addington, director of the Bureau of Control. A fat man with puffy, sadistic eyes which he hid behind thick lenses. A red toupee, obvious in its false youthfulness, replaced his lost hair.

Beside Addington sat Rafe Newton, whose youth fitted the pale reddish cast of his hair. Someday he might have eyes like his uncle, Helmut Glass—hard and unforgiving—and a fat body like his fifth cousin, Loren Addington. Now he had the look of a hungry wolf waiting for one of his pack mates to stumble.

"It's the biggest movement we've ever encountered," said Glass. He dropped into the chair at his desk. "And we don't have a single line into it. I can sense the size of it. Those couriers. Men have to be strongly indoctrinated to give up their lives." He looked up into Addington's owlish eyes. "What about the packages they carried?"

Addington fumbled in his pocket, pulled out a pill

which he popped into his mouth. "They appear to have been tri-di reels, but there wasn't enough left to reconstruct."

"Where'd they get the incendiaries?" demanded Glass.

"I don't know." Addington chewed placidly on his pill.

"You don't know." Glass mimicked Addington's tone. The fat man did not change expression. "Do you know anything?"

Addington swallowed the pill. "A rumor."

"What, what is it?"

"You call Movius?"

Glass scowled. "And there's another loose end. You haven't found him yet." He seemed at the breaking point of exasperation.

"There's a rumor going around the Warrens that he's the new boss of the Sep movement."

"Well, trace the rumor," said Glass.

"Haven't had any luck."

Glass turned to Newton. "What about you, Rafe?"

Newton's eyes took on a glaze of familial cordiality. "I've been too busy working on Gerard."

"I believe we'd better hold off on Gerard," said Glass. "Let it ride for awhile and concentrate on the Seps. Make a few surprise raids at random. Shake down the Warrens. Haul in some people for special questioning. I don't think we have much . . ."

"But I'm almost ready to move on Gerard," said Newton. His eyes had regained some of their wolfish look.

"Oh? How close?"

"Another two weeks. We're working on his male secretary now."

"Too long," said Glass. He turned back to Addington, missed the quick light of anger in Newton's eyes. "I want this thing smashed. Don't bother checking that rumor about Movius. Just find him and dump him in the river. And don't take . . ."

A door at the end of the office opened. Cecelia Lang stood in the doorway. She wore a pair of shimmering black Top Rank coveralls cut to display her figure. "Helmut," she said, her voice keyed to the tone she knew made Glass squirm.

"Just a few minutes," said Glass.

"But you said you wouldn't be long."

Newton's lips twitched into a smile, quickly erased.

"It'll just be a few seconds now," said Glass.

Cecelia waited in the doorway.

Glass turned back to the two men on the couch. "Find that man and get rid of him." He stood up, strode toward Cecelia.

"I don't like to be kept waiting," said Cecelia, taking his arm.

"I know you don't dear," said The Coor. "I'm sorry, but it was some important business. Now let's go to . . ."

They passed out of sight and hearing. Newton turned a grin on fifth cousin Loren Addington, sobered when he received no response.

Chapter 11

On the forty-seventh day following his low-opp, Movius received orders to report to Bu-Trans. The orders came out in the District Circular without any special notice attached to them.

Movius stood in the hidden room, the paper in his hands. "They want to bring me out in the open and knock me over," he said. "I'm sure of it."

Grace, working with the duplicator on the table they had installed in a corner of the room, missed catching a card as the machine disgorged it. The other cards piled up, jamming, until she shut down the machine.

Quilliam London, who always seemed to make it a point to be present when Grace was in the room, sat on Movius' cot, writing in a notebook. "We've made good preparations," he said. "Gerard has heard reports about you which make him practically drool. You're the answer to his dreams."

Movius balled the District Circular into a crumpled wad, threw it into the corner.

"It's not the ALP," said Quilliam. "It's Bu-Trans."

"Target practice for The Coor's thuggees," said Movius.

"It's early yet," said Quilliam London. "You and Grace had better go down to District Housing and ask for quarters."

Movius stared at him. "Why, I hadn't . . ."

"You'll have to make it look good," said London. "They won't be expecting you to come right out there tonight." There was a touch of grimness at the corners of his lean mouth. "The honeymoon is over."

The transport whined to a stop at the corner, waited while the morning's human cargo jostled and pushed abroad, a mood of impatient anger about them. The standard aroma of the standard breakfast puffed out on their breaths. Another LP, Daniel Movius, allowed himself to be crushed into the transport, found a space as far back as he could push. Furtive glances at his companions showed nothing he could mark as unusual. He could only assume that Bu-Con and The Coor had not had men watching District Housing, that they had not expected a hunted man to come out openly and register.

It had been a strange experience at District Housing. The clerk, with that nervous officiousness of those with petty powers, had grumbled about his paper work, assigned them quarters half a mile from Quilliam London's apartment. Grace had held Movius' arm as they'd stood there. When they were back in the street, she'd said, "We'd better go out there now. Get off the streets."

It was a standard Warren apartment—F5MC—floor 5, married couple. Two rooms nine by ten, double bed, sitting room with couch and chair, standard wall TV, collapsible table and a smoking stand. The bathroom was four by four, closet five by four. More space for the wedded; marriage had to have some advantages.

Movius tested the springs on the couch. "It'll do. You take the bedroom."

Grace opened the door between the rooms, suddenly fled into the bedroom. Movius caught a fleeting glimpse of her contorted face; he jumped up, followed. "What's wrong?"

She was drying her eyes on a corner of a blanket. "Nothing."

"Well, it's obviously something."

"I guess it's just that this is so different from what I'd imagined." She looked around her with an empty expression.

Movius found himself remembering the wedding ceremony, his desperate feeling of wrongness. "I'm sorry. I guess there are some things we didn't consider."

"Such as?" She sniffled.

"Human feelings maybe." He shrugged. "But it can't be helped." He felt like an executive telling his secretary he was sorry she couldn't have the night off but there was all this work to do. He remembered all the hours Grace had worked beside him, ignoring obvious fatigue. Movius walked into the bedroom, patted her shoulder, "Believe me, if there was some other way . . ."

She pulled away and suddenly, without warning, turned on him, eyes glittering with tears. "Of course there's no other way as long as you're filled with hate for that egotistical drive for revenge." She fell silent, put a hand to her mouth. "I'm sorry. I didn't . . ."

Again he had that feeling of being cheated, of missing something. Rather stiffly, he said, "I thought it was what you wanted, too."

Grace looked at the floor, turned her back on him. "Yes, of course.

He stepped closer, disturbed, put his hands on her shoulders. Her hair gave off a faint fragrance. The memory of that tremulous kiss came back to him. She leaned back slightly against his hands, just a faint pressure. It was enough. He had an abrupt, glaring touch of insight, thought, *Great Roper! She's in love with me!* The thought made him drop his hands, pull away. There she was, vital certainly, but really on the plain side, much too thin-featured and intense, like the ones he saw sitting in the parks on festival days, listening to ancient music. The wrong kind of fire inside to attract him. It was tragic when he thought about it.

He said, "These aren't times for anything but hate."

She sighed. "No. I guess not."

They had gone to their separate rooms, Movius to twist and turn on the too-short couch, tortured by one word in Grace's accusation — *egotistical.* He thought, *All I want is a clean government for everyone.* And far back in his mind something sniggered and said, "With you at the top!"

The transport turned on the parkway — Government Avenue — began making frequent stops to disgorge writhing blobs of workers. Movius saw his stop coming, worked his way forward, was squeezed out with the rest into the chill morning air.

There was the building: Bu-Trans. A towering concrete hive, its tiled floors clicking to purposeful feet. A container for efficient scurrying hither and yon, papers clutched in hands. Machines clacking and buzzing, pneumo-tubes whacking out their cartridges with more bits of paper. A sum total of officiousness.

Movius joined the inbound stream of workers, broke away in the cavernous lobby to go to the window labeled STARTING CLERK. The clerk's tired eyes peered out of a steel wicket. "Name and number?"

"Daniel Movius, 662843509, LP."

The clerk turned to check the records. Movius

leaned on the counter to wait, became conscious of two men, one standing on either side of him. Something hard pressed against his left side. He looked down, saw a fap gun in the hand of the man on his left.

"Daniel Movius?" asked the one on the right.

"Yes." Movius looked at the man, mind churning. This was what he had feared. He said, "Why?"

"We'll ask the questions." The man began patting Movius' pockets, stooped to feel along his legs. Presently, he stood up, said, "He's not carrying it."

The pressure was removed from Movius' left side.

"Where've you been, Movius?" asked the man on the right.

"With my wife," said Movius, forcing his voice to remain even and questioning. "We've been on our honeymoon. I . . ."

The starting clerk returned to the window. "You report to Department CR-14." He suddenly noticed the two men beside Movius. "You must take your places in line," he said. "We serve everybody in his proper turn."

The man on the right flashed a badge and identification card. "Bu-Con," he said. "This man is a fugitive from work report."

The clerk gave a glance to the badge and card, glanced down to papers he held in his hand. "I don't see how that can be. I have his work order here in my hand. It came through yesterday. He's reporting well within the forty-eight-hour limit." The clerk reached out, grasped Movius' thumb, held thumb and papers under the facsimile-eye on his counter. "Same man."

"We'll tell you if it's the same man or not," said the one on Movius' right.

The clerk leaned forward, said, "Look, bull-con, I've identified this man as one assigned to CR-14. I'm going to call them upstairs and report what's going on." He pulled a phone from beneath the counter, put it to his ear.

The man on Movius' left rested his fap-gun on the counter, said, "Put away the phone, sonny."

"If you pull that trigger, the guard in our tower will drop you in your tracks," said the clerk. "We don't trust you bull-con illegitimates over here in Bu-Trans." He bent over the phone. "Get me Mr. Gerard, will you, beautiful? I'll wait."

"Movius is going with us," said the man on the right.

"That may be," said the clerk. "But I'm reporting this to the top all the same." Again he moved the phone closer to his mouth. "Mr. Gerard?" He waited. "Mr. Gerard? This is Bailey downstairs. Daniel Movius, the new CR-14, just reported and there are a couple of bull-cons here threatening to take him away on a charge of failure to report." A rasping sound issued from the phone. "Sure it's a phony," said the clerk.

The man on Movius' right said, "Let's go." He took Movius' arm, turned him around. "Out the door and don't give us any trouble."

The clerk tipped the phone away from his mouth. "The big boss says for you to wait."

"We don't take our orders from your boss," said the one with the gun.

The clerk reached under the counter. A clanging crash sounded from the front doors as a steel barrier dropped. "You're not going anywhere," said the clerk. "Not unless you happened to bring an oxy-torch in your side pocket."

The man with the gun looked to his companion. "We can't do it in here," he said. "They'd blast us first and ask questions later."

"I'm thinking," said the other man.

They mean to kill me! thought Movius. He suddenly slashed his right hand down at the gunman's wrist, heard the gun clatter on the floor. Almost in the same motion, he brought up his left thumb, jamming it behind the other man's ear, saw him collapse. Again he thanked fate for the years spent in the privileged gymnasiums, for Okashi's patient teaching. The gunman was bending to pick up his weapon. Movius stepped back half a step, kicked the man alongside the head. The man sprawled forward onto his face. Movius stooped, picked up the gun, walked back to the clerk's window. "They were going to kill me," he said.

The clerk was speaking rapidly into the phone. "Yes. Now he has the gun . . . Well, I don't really know. It happened so fast I couldn't follow it . . . Yes, I'll have him sent right up . . . Yes, it's the same man for CR-14."

Movius put the fap gun on the counter. "What do I do with this?"

"Leave it right there," said the clerk. "I'll give it to him when he wakes up. You're to report to the big boss." He leaned through the wicket, pointed to his left. "Take that elevator all the way to the top—seventy-first floor. They're expecting you." He shook his head. "Man! That was beautiful."

The elevator let him out in a penthouse office, sunlight glaring into the place from too many windows. A male receptionist built like a Roman gladiator, even to the beaked nose, said "You the one snowed under the two bull-cons?"

Movius nodded.

The Roman gladiator hooked a thumb over his shoulder. "Go right in. You're welcome."

Venetian blinds made the inner office gloomy after the reception room. Gerard, a frail-bodied man with a bald head two sizes too large for his body, was sitting with his back to the door, speaking into a Dictaphone. As Movius entered, he put down the Dictaphone, swiveled his chair. Gerard had dishwater blue eyes with lids which gave the impression of a chicken's nictating membrane.

"Well, so you're . . ." Gerard stopped, stared intently at Movius. "I should pay more attention," he said. "I didn't put the name and face together." He sat back, waved Movius to a chair across from him. "You're the Daniel Movius who went out with Liaison a month or so ago."

"That's right." Movius dropped into the chair.

Gerard wriggled in his chair and a glistening reflection of him in the polished surface of the desk matched the movement. "What happened?"

What could he tell this man? Movius wondered. Gerard was one of the top twenty-five in government and, by all the stories, a powerful and ruthless man. Movius decided on partial truth, said, "The Coor wanted my fiancée."

"Oh?" Gerard's voice became distant.

Movius wondered if he had overplayed his hand, cursed himself for not thinking twice. Both Quilliam London and O'Brien had said Gerard hated The Coor, though.

"The Coor, eh?" said Gerard.

"Glass didn't realize I was tired of her and looking for a way out," said Movius. "When he took her off my hands, I married the woman I wanted."

Gerard leaned forward, a half-smile on his face. "What's this about failing to report?"

Play it cautiously, thought Movius. "I'm sure I don't know," he said. "I waited until my number came up—I saw it last night—and reported as soon as I could."

Gerard leaned back, pulled a phone from a recess in his desk, spoke into it. "Get me old owl guts Addington at Bu-Con."

It's what O'Brien and London said, thought Movius. *They hate each other at the top.*

Gerard stretched the muscles of his neck, wriggled in his chair. "Hello, is that you, owl guts?" he asked. "The same to you. What do you want with my new CR-14, Daniel Movius?" He waited, jerked his head up, glancing furtively at Movius. "Is that so? Well, that's penalty service. What was the charge?" Another wait. "Can't find it, eh? Maybe you'd better learn how to keep records over there." Gerard wore a fierce grin. "Sure, I know where he is. He's sitting right across from me . . . Sure, you can question him; right here in my office and no place else. And that's final." He paused listening, put a hand over the mouthpiece. "Somebody's just telling him about his two flunkies you messed up." Gerard turned back to the phone. "He did? Well isn't that a shame? Why don't you patch them up and bring them along for another go at him?" Gerard listened, said, "Goodbye, owl guts," slammed down the receiver. He turned the fierce grin on Movius. "If you're clean, Movius, I'll throw everything I have behind you. I like nothing better than cobbing old owl guts. But you'd just better be clean. They won't dare touch you if I'm behind you."

I only hope you're right, thought Movius. He said, "I don't know what the hell this is all about."

"They're on their way over," said O'Brien.

Movius framed a mental picture of Addington

going to the elevator, riding down, getting into his car, driving the two blocks to Bu-Trans, coming up the elevator here. Almost to the second when he felt they should arrive, Gladiator ushered the visitors into Gerard's office. Addington did look like an owl — fat, dumpy body, round face, horn-rimmed glasses and a thin, pinched nose. He was accompanied by two men. With a start, Movius recognized a murderous glare. The other was an aide carrying a bulging briefcase.

"Before we get off to any wrong starts," said Gerard, "maybe I should remind everybody that no one gets out of this building alive without my say-so." He rubbed a hand across his bald head.

Addington sat down with a grunt, popped a white lozenge into his mouth. "Save the drama for those who appreciate it, bulb head." The two aides remained standing. Addington had not shown that he even knew Movius was present. Suddenly, he whirled on Movius, said, "What we really want you for is murder!"

Movius did not have to feign surprise. He looked from Addington to Gerard, back to Addington. "This is fantastic. I've been on my honeymoon. I don't know what you're talking about."

Without taking his eyes from Movius, the Bu-Con chief reached up to his aide, took the briefcase, opened it on his lap. From the case he pulled a paper, glanced at it. "On the eve of Mid-summer Festival, you, Daniel Movius, in the company with another man as yet unidentified, did accost Howell Pescado and Birch Morfon in the Richmond Warrenate. You and companion did then attack Mr. Pescado and Mr. Morfon with such violence that Mr. Pescado died. You then stole Mr. Pescado's gun and with it did wound Benjam Rousch, who had stopped to investigate the disturbance."

Movius shook his head. "I've never heard of these people. I've never been in such a fight."

Gerard leaned forward. The reflected image on the desk surface darted with him. "To hell with a street brawl! What's this about Dan failing to report for the ALP?"

Movius noted the use of his first name and knew the familiarity was aimed at making Addington unsure of their relationship.

Addington flushed, spoke without looking up from the paper. "That was an error. He is not wanted on such a charge."

Gerard said, "Oh?" He leaned back, turned to Movius. "Did you knock over this Pescado?"

"No."

"You say you've been on your honeymoon," said Addington. "Isn't it a fact that you were hiding out instead?"

"Hiding from what?" asked Movius. He shrugged. "I have been staying pretty close to my bride, of course; except to come out and register my opps."

Addington hunted through the briefcase, extracted another paper. "That's another thing, Movius. You registered opps everywhere from Killson Warrenate to Lascadou."

"Is there a law that says you have to register some special place?" asked Movius.

"You were never in these places," said Addington.

"How do you know?" asked Movius.

"Because we . . ." Addington broke off.

Movius smiled. He thought of Gerard's obvious hate for this man, decided to burn his bridges and play all out for Gerard. It was not difficult to put hate into his tone. "Look, you fat son-of-a-bitch!" he barked.

"I've had all I'm taking from you! I've spent twelve years in the service of the government. Never once taken my off-time, always registered my opps, kept my nose clean. Two of your trained hounds put a gun on me downstairs and talked about killing me. I don't know why I'm your target, but I'm telling you now to look out!" He glanced at the man he had thumbed. The aide had been edging toward Movius. "And if your brother here moves another inch toward me I'll wipe up this office with him!" The aide took another involuntary step backwards.

"Put up or shut up," said Gerard. "Unless you can prove your charges, I'm backing Dan all the way."

Movius took a deep breath.

Addington glared at Gerard. "I have two witnesses."

"No good." Gerard shook his head. "Your friends know too much about lying. This has to be tied down with fingerprints, full laboratory evidence."

"I saw him myself!" raged Addington.

"You're an even bigger liar," said Gerard.

Addington's face went purple. "I suppose Movius has been put through ocamine so he can take a lie-detector test without a quiver?"

"I wouldn't know," said Gerard. "LD evidence won't hold with me, anyway." Gerard was obviously enjoying himself.

Addington leaned forward, face flushed. "You know this man is guilty! You're just aiding him to spite me! I'm warning you . . ."

A buzzing sounded from beneath the desk, interrupting him. Gerard answered his phone, passed it across to Addington. "It's for you, owl guts."

Addington snatched the phone, said, "Yes, this is

Addington." He listened, smiled. "You have? Well, hold her there." He passed the phone back to Gerard, still smiling, turned to Movius. "We have your bride. You're coming with us now or else."

Movius felt himself go almost blank. It was as though he watched another man rise slowly from his chair, take two steps toward Addington. The aide moved to cut him off.

"Movius!" It was Gerard's voice.

The sharp tone of command restored some of Movius' control. *I got Grace into this,* he thought. *I can't let them harm her. What can I do?*

"Well?" asked Addington.

Movius fought to control his thoughts. *How can I fight them?* A desperate gamble flashed through his mind. He turned, walked around behind Gerard's desk. From an inner pocket he withdrew his stylus, unscrewed the back cap, exposing the sharp edge of the re-load. Grasping Gerard's hand, he made a short scratch on the back.

"Ouch!" Gerard put the hand to his mouth, darted his other hand toward a pocket.

Movius shook his head, put the stylus to his mouth, blew on it. Quietly, he capped the stylus, waited while he counted silently to fifteen. Addington and his aides were staring at him puzzled.

"I have just released a quantity of high-dispersion poison gas in this room sufficient to kill five hundred people," said Movius. "Mr. Gerard and myself are immunized. In thirty minutes you three will die in agony, every muscle of your bodies tearing violently." He put the stylus back in his inside pocket.

Addington jumped to his feet, leaned across the desk, bellowed at Gerard, "Stop this madman!"

Gerard leaned back. "Why should I? I won't be harmed."

One of Gerard's hands remained beneath the desk. "And if you make a move to come around this desk, you'll die much more quickly."

"You have thirty minutes in which to bring my wife up here unharmed," said Movius. "In fact, if the antidote is to have the time to work, you have less than that. About fifteen minutes is all."

Gerard pushed the telephone across the desk. "I'd make the call if I were you."

"He's bluffing," said Addington in a faint voice.

"I wouldn't count on that," said Gerard.

"I *have* heard of such a gas," said Addington slowly.

"Bu-Trans has many resources," said Gerard.

"So that's the way it is?" said Addington. Face pale, he took up the phone. "Get me Pearsons at Bu-Con." He waited. "Ev, bring the Movius woman over to Bu-Trans right away. Don't ask questions; just bring her! Come right on up to bulb-head's office with her." He slammed the phone onto the desk, sat down.

Gerard quietly replaced the phone on its hook.

"The first thing you notice is your heart beating more rapidly and much stronger," said Movius. "You become very aware of your heartbeat."

The aide who had carried the briefcase suddenly paled, swayed, sat down in a hard-backed chair against the wall. He began to draw in deep breaths.

"Some people don't have as high a tolerance as others," said Movius. He noticed that both Addington and the other aide were forcing in deep breaths. The seated aide suddenly pitched forward to the floor with a loud thump.

Movius smiled. *A little applied psychology plus a weak*

will equals a fainting spell, he thought. *Now they're convinced.*

Addington jumped to his feet. "Give me that antidote! I'm a sick man! I can already feel my heart pounding!"

"When my wife gets here," said Movius. "Not before."

"Sit down," said Gerard. "Exertion only makes the poison work faster."

Addington slumped back into his chair, fumbled in a pocket, brought out a white pill which he put onto his tongue with a shaking hand. He flopped the pill into his mouth, gulped it. "You're going to answer for this," he said. He looked toward the door. "I should have told him to hurry." He glanced at his wristwatch.

A knock sounded on the door. "Come in," said Gerard.

The gladiator for the outer office appeared in the doorway, his bulk obscuring the view of whoever was behind him.

"Everybody come in," said Gerard.

Gladiator stepped into the room, followed by Grace and a chunky, vapid-faced man with sadistic eyes. Grace—wrapped in a blanket, hair disheveled—had a short scratch on one cheek. Her eyes blazed fury. She shook herself free of vapid-face's detaining hand, suddenly saw Movius. "Dan!"

"Everything's all right, dear," said Movius. He went around the desk, put an arm around her shoulders. "Did they harm you?"

She shook her head. "They were searching me." She turned. "That creature and another one."

Vapid-face licked his lips. "Nice," he said, leering at Movius.

"You have your wife," said Addington. "Give us the antidote."

"You're all breathing a poison gas for which Mr. Movius has the only antidote," said Gerard, looking at vapid-face.

"Well?" said Addington.

"First put all your weapons on Mr. Gerard's desk," said Movius.

"See here!" said Addington.

"Do as he says!" barked Gerard, voice harsh.

Movius took out his stylus, made a minute scratch on the back of Grace's hand, did the same for the gladiator.

"On the desk," said Movius. He capped the stylus, put it away, began patting Addington's pockets, stooped to feel along his legs. The Bu-Con chief wore one tiny fap gun strapped to an ankle and two others in pocket holsters. His gunman aide also had one on the ankle and two in the pockets. The clerk had one in a lapel holster. Vapid-face wore a poison dart stutter gun hanging from a shoulder strap inside his suit. A crease concealed the slit by which it could be brought out quickly.

Gerard's eyes widened when he saw the weapon. "That's outlawed," he said.

"So it's outlawed," said Addington peevishly. "So's poison gas."

Movius put the weapons on the desk. Gerard swept them all into a drawer.

Movius bent over the unconscious clerk on the floor, made a deep slash in the back of the man's hand with the sharp tip of the stylus. The clerk moaned, began to stir. Movius went to the gunman. Addington stepped forward. "I have to have that immediately!"

"After him," said Movius.

Addington quivered, his eyes glittering behind the thick glasses.

Movius made a deep slash in the aide's hand, grabbed Addington's hand, made an even deeper slash. Vapid-face stepped forward, held out his hand. Movius ignored him, capped the stylus and put it back in his pocket.

"What about me?" the man asked.

Movius turned to Grace. "Are you sure they didn't harm you?"

She blushed, broke off, and began to cry silently, bringing her hands from beneath the blanket to cover her face.

"What about me?" vapid-face repeated.

Movius' face hardened. "You don't get it."

Addington whirled on Gerard. "You can't let him just . . ."

"Dan is one of my most trusted aides," said Gerard. "I give him a free hand in these matters. If he doesn't think Ev should live, then I go by his judgment. Personally, I'm inclined to agree with him in this instance."

Vapid-face pushed through the group, leaned against Gerard's desk, face contorted. "You can't do this to me!"

"You're mistaken," said Gerard coldly. "We're doing it."

The man sank to his knees, clutching the edge of the desk. "Please! Look! I'm begging you!"

Movius suddenly felt sickened.

"Give it to him" said Grace.

The man turned his contorted face toward her. "Thank you."

Movius brought out the stylus, uncapped it, bent

and slashed the kneeling man across the cheek. "I want to recognize you next time! If you so much as look cross-eyed at my wife ever again I'll get you and you can beg until your voice runs dry!"

Vapid-face stood up, hand against his bleeding cheek.

The clerk on the floor again stirred, lifting his head. He got to his feet, looked around vacantly.

Movius said, "All right, get out of here!"

The gladiator opened the door, stood aside.

Addington turned a measuring stare on Movius. "I'm going to remember your face . . . personally!"

Gerard leaned forward, his bald head glistening as brightly as the desk top. "Let's understand something. If anything is done to Dan or his wife because of what happened here, I will consider it was done to me." His eyes slitted. "If you want open war, owl guts, you'll get it."

Without a word, Addington turned, went out, trailed by his three aides. Gerard's receptionist closed the door.

Movius went to Grace, helped her into a chair, pulled the blanket around her knees. "We'll send out for some clothes."

"I'll get them from our supplies," said Gerard. He picked up the phone, gave terse orders, replaced the phone. Turning to Movius, he said, "I want you to give the lab the formula for that poison gas and antidote. They could come in handy. And while you're at it, you could tell me where you got them."

Movius took out his stylus, tossed it onto the desk. "What poison gas? That's a standard stylus."

Gerard picked it up, examined it.

"I once got a nasty scratch from the sharp end of a

re-load," said Movius. "I remembered it and the fact that I'd heard a story about a poison gas. Come to think about it, I read about the gas in one of Navvy's pop-mags. It was fiction."

Gerard looked at the scratch on his hand.

"Sorry about that," said Movius. "That was the convincer."

Suddenly, Gerard jerked back in his chair, began to laugh. The bellowing of it filled the office. "Ohhhhh," he said. "Ohhhhh, the look on Addington's face! Ohhhhh. And the way you made him wait until the last!" It was a full minute before Gerard could control himself. He took out a handkerchief, dabbed at his eyes. "Movius, I would have let you cut half through my hand for that show." He replaced the handkerchief, sat forward.

Grace was looking from one to the other, puzzled. "What . . ."

Movius shook his head.

"Movius, I've been looking for a man like you for a long time. I saw the sorter card and could see from it that you were good. But that was as resourceful a bit of quick thinking as I've ever seen." Again he chuckled. "I have a little job . . ."

A knock sounded on the door.

"Yes?"

Gladiator appeared with a bundle. Gerard stood up, went around the desk and took the bundle. The receptionist closed the door. Gerard opened another door in the side wall, revealing a small room with a leather couch. "You can dress in here, Mrs. Movius."

Grace stood up, pulling the blanket around herself. "Thank you." She went into the room.

Gerard tossed the package onto the couch, closed

the door, returned to his desk, sat down. He took out a handkerchief, patted at the perspiration on his bald head. "You've got good taste, Movius." He put away the handkerchief. "She's no raving beauty, but she has good looks and personality, the kind that wear well as a wife." Gerard glanced down to Movius' stylus on the desk. "Oh, yes — the job."

Movius hitched his chair closer to the desk.

"Just a minute," said Gerard. He took the phone, said, "Get me the Sorter cards on Daniel Movius. Bailey has them downstairs." Presently, something went *Pop!* under the desk. Gerard reached down, brought up the pneumo-tube cartridge, opened it, pulled out the cards.

"That could be dangerous," said Movius.

Gerard looked up from the cards. "What?"

"How do you know what's coming up in that tube?"

Gerard pulled back from his desk, looked under it. "Great Gallup! I never thought of that! It could just as easily be a charge of nitrox!" He moved his chair around beside the desk, went on reading the cards. Presently, he looked up, put the cards on his desk, his expression thoughtful. He ran a hand over his bald head, looked at Movius.

"I was just refreshing my memory. The records show that you ran one of the most efficient departments of the government. Also, you have an extremely high loyalty index." He looked at the cards. "Extremely high."

That was the old *Daniel Movius,* he thought. *Now we get the bid for that loyalty.*

"I've just saved your life," said Gerard. "Do you know that?"

Movius nodded. "And I may have saved yours." He

looked across the desk toward the hidden tube.

Gerard wet his lips with his tongue. "Exactly. I wasn't joking when I said I've been looking for someone like you. I need a man I can trust like my right arm."

"Tell me what to do," said Movius.

Gerard sat back. "In a bureau such as this you sometimes get someone who is overly ambitious." His expression hardened. "Owl Guts Addington and The Coor are behind the man who heads one of my sections. They hope to put that man in my seat." He mopped nervously at his bald head. "There have been two attempts on my life."

"And you want a bodyguard?" asked Movius.

"No, much more than that. You were certified to department CR-14 by the Sorter. I want you to go down there and hang a frame around the neck of the department director. I know you're the man for the job."

Why all the praise? wondered Movius. He decided to apply London's methods, get at what the other man wanted. "What's so dangerous about the job?"

"Mmmmm," said Gerard. "You are sharp." He slapped a hand onto the desk. "All right, here's the proposition. You're filling a vacancy in the department caused by the death of the last man I sent down there. He fell down a light well."

Movius nodded, pointed toward Gerard's desk drawer. "Let me have that lapel gun."

Gerard leaned back, opened the drawer, handed gun and holster to Movius.

"What is CR-14?" asked Movius.

"Confidential routing," said Gerard.

We're playing it cagey, thought Movius. He said, "Who's the department head?"

"Rafe Newton. He's a cousin of The Coor."

"Nepotism?"

"It sometimes happens," said Gerard. "I'd boot him in a minute otherwise." He leaned back, steepled his hands. "No love lost on The Coor, is there?"

Movius shook his head.

"I believe The Coor is heading for a showdown at the time of his major poll this Fall." Gerard consulted a desk calendar. "That's October 8, about two weeks away." He looked up at Movius from beneath his brows. "You were tired of this latest plaything Glass picked up, eh?" Almost to himself he said, "I'll have to see he finds that out."

The door to Gerard's private room swung open. Grace emerged wearing a standard work suit, a little too large for her. The legs had been rolled up.

Without looking at her Gerard said, "You were listening, weren't you, my dear?"

Grace's voice had a tone of defiance. "Why not?"

Gerard turned his bald head slowly until he was facing her. "No reason. A wife should take an interest in what's happening to her husband." He reached into the desk drawer, withdrew one of the ankle guns, slipped gun and handful of recharges from the holster. Coming around the desk, he displayed the little weapon to Grace. "You slip the re-charge in like this. Then press this to break the seal and put the first pellet in the chamber. This is the safety. When it shows red the gun is ready to fire." He handed it to Grace, turned toward the open door of his private room. "Put a pellet into the couch there to get the feel of it. I want you to have this gun in case they try to pick you up again."

Grace lifted the little weapon, squeezed off a single shot. It went *fap SPLAT!* into the leather couch. She thumbed on the safety, put the gun in her pocket.

Gerard leaned back on his desk. "You've fired one of those before." Suddenly, he bent forward from the hips. "Where?"

Grace looked to Movius, eyes frightened.

"I said where does an LP female learn to shoot a fap gun?" Gerard demanded.

"I showed her," said Movius.

Gerard continued to stare at Grace. "Where did you get the gun, Movius?"

Here it is, thought Movius. He said, "Off Pescado."

Gerard whirled toward him.

"He was one of The Coor's bully boys," said Movius. "He jumped me the same night I was low-opped. He and two others."

"You were running away from that ALP wrong rap?"

Movius shrugged. "What else could I do?"

"And they had six weeks to find you and couldn't? Where'd you hide?" His voice bit off the questions as though he was shooting them from a gun.

Movius nodded toward Grace. "My wife hid me."

Gerard moved slowly away from the desk, turned to look at Movius. "I understand that will have to do for now."

Movius got to his feet.

Gerard looked at the muscular bulk of him, said almost to himself. "I don't think they'll be dropping you down any light wells. No, indeed, I don't." His eyes stared up at Movius. "You clean this one up and I've a better job for you." He turned, reached across the desk, opened a top drawer, pulled out a green pad. Using Movius' stylus, he scribbled on it, finished, looked at the stylus and grinned. "Mind if I keep this as a sort of memento?"

"Not at all."

Gerard pocketed the stylus, handed the note to Movius. "This presented at District Housing will get you an apartment in the privileged section—a special apartment where you'll be safe. My own quarters are on the roof. I'll have a car and driver assigned to you. We may as well come out in the open; there's no way to keep your position secret after what happened today. You'll go into CR-14 as my man and no questions asked." Gerard waved a hand. "Take the rest of the day; report in the morning."

"Will there be any trouble about the special status?" asked Movius. "The Sorter rated me clerk."

"And I rated you executive assistant," said Gerard. "That's a bureau chief's privilege."

"Let's get my duties straight," said Movius. He looked down at the District Housing order in his hand.

"I don't want to know what you do," said Gerard. "You get rid of Newton. Either make it legal or make it look accidental." He turned to Grace. "I'll have you taken off the LP rolls."

"You needn't bother."

Movius could tell from her tone that she'd formed a violent dislike for Gerard.

"You're coming off the rolls anyway," said Gerard. "Can't have Dan worrying about his wife. You stick close to the apartment. I've a small army of guards on the place. You'll be safe there." He turned away, dismissing them.

As they went out the door, they heard Gerard on the phone. "Have a car and driver in the side driveway for Mr. Movius. And send up some building maintenance men. I want my pneumo tube yanked out and re-routed into the outer office."

Chapter 12

"And *you* were almost ready to get rid of Gerard?" said Glass. He leaned back against his desk, stared down at Rafe Newton.

The nephew avoided The Coor's eyes. "I could . . ."

"You can leave Gerard alone!" Glass barked the words. "And you can get a sample of that poison gas for us. Gerard is suddenly too bold. I want to know how long Movius has been working for him. Probably all the time he was Liaitor. He could have booby traps in every department of government; he went everywhere. That gas! How could someone develop a thing like that right under our noses? That may be what's making Gerard so bold."

"Or desperate," said Newton.

"I said *bold*." Glass frowned. "We have to find out what his position is before we make a move."

Newton shifted his position on the couch, "What about Movius?"

"Movius! Well, we know where he is now. Give Movius a couple of days to rattle around while we check back on everyone who contacts him. Then kill him." Glass smiled without humor.

"And the new wife?"

"Leave her alone until you get rid of Movius. But pick up her father and the brother. The brother used to drive for Movius. That must be where he met the woman."

Newton lowered his eyes. "The father and brother have disappeared."

Glass lost his temper. "People can't just disappear! Find them! You hear me? Drag in the wife . . ."

"I thought you said to leave her alone?" Newton sounded like a small boy objecting to a reprimand.

The Coor calmed himself, tightened his lips into a thin line. "So I did. Let that stand."

"Okay, but . . ."

"Drag her in for questioning after you get Movius. Get your information." Glass raised his voice to a roar. "And don't let him slip through your fingers again!"

Chapter 13

The apartment was higher on the hill than the Third Rank quarters he had occupied before the low-opp. There was a feeling of silence, isolation in the new apartment never found in a Warren. And space. No sensation of the walls creeping closer with each passing day. The china clinked with a more refined tone. The blankets rustled more softly. Workers spoke in hushed undertones.

Grace came out of the bedroom with its twin beds and subtly richer furnishings. She scuffed a toe against the thick pile of the living room rug. Movius was sitting in one of the deep chairs looking out the floor-to-ceiling windows at the city.

"There's a kitchen," she said. "A dining room and a private kitchen-service tube if we want the regular meals. And the bathroom must be ten feet square. It has a tub." She sat down on the arm of Movius' chair.

"The privileges of the High-Opp," said Movius. "There's another one, too. We have a master scrambler on the roof. No spy beams can look in on the High-Opp." He glanced up at her. "We don't have to pretend we're making love here. We can talk right out."

She blushed.

"Where did you learn to shoot a fap gun?" he demanded.

She slipped from the chair arm, stood up, walked away from him. "My father taught me."

"Your father has never . . ." He broke off, wondering if that were true.

She whirled on him. "My mother was killed in the educator riots! My father fought his way out with a stolen gun to save us! He still has it!"

So Grace had lost her mother the way he'd lost his. How the rioters had enjoyed killing the women, the breeders. He said, "I'm sorry. My mother got it the same way. I never knew her." His voice had flat undertones.

"They didn't tell me," she said.

"They? Who are they?"

"I mean my father."

The old bean pole? he thought. He said, "How would your father know?"

"He made inquiries."

"Oh."

So they had made inquiries. He let the silence grow cold between them. Grace returned to the arm of his chair.

"Why is Gerard putting an untried man into a tough spot?" he asked.

"You're not exactly untried," she said. "He has your Sorter record and he saw you in action today. Remember that."

"He may be in a shakier position than he lets on," said Movius. "He mentioned two attempts on his life." He lifted himself from the chair, paced across the room and back, clenching and unclenching his fists. "But this is like grabbing at straws."

She stood, walked to the window, turned around, silhouetted against the view of the city, her face in shadow. "Dan, please be careful."

Her words touched off a flash of anger in his. She would have to go all female on him at a time like this. "Mind your own business!" he snapped.

Her eyes widened, she turned, ran into the bedroom. He heard the bathroom door slam, water turned on full force. Even above the noise of the water he could hear her sobs.

He flung himself into the chair and stared at nothing. *And why do I keep thinking about the helpless way she looked at me today, standing there in Gerard's office in that blanket?* He gritted his teeth. *And why did I get so angry because another man saw Grace unclothed?* An isolated fragment of the wedding ceremony flitted through his mind, " . . .to cherish and to protect . . ."

Grace returned, stood in the doorway. Movius thrust his hands into his pockets to still their restless movements.

"Do we have any sleeping pills?" she asked. Her voice gave only a faint hint of the tears.

"I don't know. Why?"

"I haven't been sleeping well lately. There are none in the bathroom."

"High-Opp apartments should come equipped with sleeping tablets," he said. "Send out for some. Phone's over there in the hall."

"Would you go down to the servo-mat in the lobby and get me some?" she asked. "It would be quicker."

The request coincided with his feelings. He felt he had to get away from the apartment, be by himself to think. He couldn't think with her standing there staring at him.

"I'll get them," he said. He got to his feet, walked past her to the hall door without looking at her.

She stopped him at the door. "Dan."

He waited, hand on the knob. "Yes?"

"Thank you for saving me from Bu-Con. I know it would have been much simpler just to let them have me."

"I was lucky." Then he thought, *Lucky! Anyone but that fat hypochondriac Addington would have pulled a gun first and called for a showdown.*

He went out into the hall. An empty elevator stood open at his level. He stepped inside, punched for the lobby. The door closed and there was a sharp hissing sound. Instead of going down, the elevator surged upward. Movius punched the DOWN button a second time, noticed a strange tang in the air. He sniffed at it, felt the darkness sweet over him. "The Coor!" he thought. "Of all the dumb . . ."

Chapter 14

"We must give him the idea that Bu-Psych is omnipotent," said O'Brien, leaning back in his chair, steepling his fingers before his mouth. "He must grow to feel that we know every move he makes." O'Brien lowered his hands, leaned forward.

Grace stood at the end of the table, back to the chart with the single red line. The line had been carried perhaps an inch farther along its journey, rising slightly.

"I understand," she said. "It's the only way you can control him"

"I wanted a chance to talk to you, anyway," said O'Brien. He leaned back, pressed his fingers against his greying temples. "I learned today that you've been asking questions of one of our consultants."

She turned her profile to him, stared at the chart on the other wall.

O'Brien leaned forward. "Why did you ask what kind of a husband a man with a high loyalty index makes?"

"I was curious." Her tone was defiant.

"And your curiosity was satisfied? You found out they make extremely devoted husbands." He slapped his hand against the table top to startle her. "Grace! If you were called upon to eliminate him today, what would you do?"

She paled. "Maybe you'd better get somebody else."

"We can't. We don't dare arouse his suspicions."

"Then I'd have to . . . to do it," she said, her voice low. She turned, looked at O'Brien. "Nate, what is the loyalty index, really?"

"I don't know if I can answer that question in simple terms," he said. "Essentially, though, I guess you could say it measures the feeling a person has for the welfare of others."

She nodded. "Where is he?"

"Let's not get sentimental," said O'Brien. "He's under hypnos now, being examined. We want to know how he feels toward you." O'Brien leaned back.

Her hands began to tremble and she clasped them tightly together. "He's very resourceful," she said.

O'Brien looked at her hands, the knuckles so white where she clasped them. He tugged at an ear. "Yes. Now we want to know how he operates in CR-14. He knows Newton will be out to kill him as he did the other man Gerard sent down. He also knows that Gerard's threat may not keep Addington and The Coor away."

She turned a piercing stare upon him. "What do you think Dan will do?"

O'Brien glanced at the red line on the chart. "Our treatment has been pretty drastic. He has been thrown into a tough problem situation. My guess is he'll show his ruthless side. He'll stamp on Newton the way he'd stamp on an insect. Addington and The Coor, too, given the chance. It's a delicate situation, but one calculated to win Gerard's trust if he succeeds. That's what Gerard would like to do to his enemies—stamp on them—if he dared. I believe Gerard is taken in by the loyalty index. He thinks he has won Movius' loyalty. Gerard doesn't know too much about the variants on the index."

"What about my father?" she asked. "Does he have a ruthless said, too?"

"All revolutionaries have a ruthless side," he said. "They have to be practical. That means doing the thing that is necessary. Your father and brother had to go into hiding today. We had planned on it."

"Hiding?"

"You've been recognized as Mrs. Movius," said O'Brien. "Your relations, therefore, know something. They might be . . . uh, persuaded to reveal what they know."

Grace sighed, looked down at her hands.

"You have been remembering that you are a woman," said O'Brien. "You must put that memory aside. You are a Bu-Psych operative. When this is all over, the crisis past, you can find some nice young man . . ."

He watched, calculatingly, as Grace turned away, went to the door, opened it slowly. She kept her face averted as she spoke. "I'll leave now if you don't mind. We can't let him see me here when you bring him out."

"Of course."

She closed the door behind her.

O'Brien jerked to his feet, stood at the window, staring out over the city where lights were beginning to spring alive in the dusk. "Such weak tools," he whispered. "Put a little strain on one and it bends out of shape."

Chapter 15

It was the same hard pallet in the same red-walled cell. Movius sat up, put his feet over the edge. What was O'Brien trying to prove? Something Quilliam London had said came back to Movius: "Find out what the other man wants." He'd used that idea once before this day — on Gerard. All right, what did O'Brien want? Why this method of bringing him in? To make him believe that Bu-Psych was omnipotent, maybe that they could pick him up any time. But that could mean that underneath it all O'Brien was unsure. The man who knows his own strength doesn't stand around flexing his muscles. The thought gave him confidence. He got to his feet, waited until the end door opened, strode to meet O'Brien as the Bu-Psych chief entered.

"Let's talk outside," said Movius. "Your red walls have lost their potency."

O'Brien hesitated for the briefest instant. "Of course." He tossed a canvas chair onto the pallet, turned and led the way out of the cell. "My office is over here." He opened the door for Movius, followed him into the room of the charts.

Movius glanced swiftly around the room, saw the chair he knew must be O'Brien's at the end of the table, strode to it, sat down. O'Brien appeared not to notice.

"I wanted to hear from your own lips what happened with Warren Gerard today," said O'Brien. He lowered himself into the chair usually occupied by Quilliam London, unconsciously assumed London's pose of reserved superiority.

From my own lips, thought Movius. *That could mean he already has heard the story. From who? Addington? Gerard? The gladiator? One of Addington's men? Grace? But she was back at the apartment.* He glanced at the windows. Nearly dark. He had entered the elevator shortly after noon. Grace could have been here. Why had they kept him unconscious so long?

"Your report is the price of your continued freedom," said O'Brien. "Let's have the story."

Movius sat back. *The story? All right. A bare recounting.* He held out no essential details, watched the unmoving way O'Brien accepted the information. Yes, he had heard it before. Movius finished, waited.

O'Brien said, "How is your marriage with Grace London coming?"

Now why would O'Brien be interested in his married life? Out of some perverse impulse, Movius said, "We're expecting our first baby in the Spring."

He hadn't expected the reaction from O'Brien. The Bu-Psych chief jerked to attention, took two deep breaths, suddenly jumped to his feet. "I just thought of something," he said and dashed out of the room.

That hit him, thought Movius. Why?

In a moment, O'Brien returned, sat down, wiped his forehead with a handkerchief. "Important business I forgot to attend to," he said lamely.

"Let me ask a question," said Movius. "The last time I was here you spoke about a crisis. What is this crisis?"

O'Brien waited a full minute before answering, head lowered, staring upward at Movius.

I hit him hard with that remark about Grace, thought Movius. But why? What difference could it make to him?

O'Brien stirred in his chair, rubbed the greying temples with the tips of his fingers. "Our civilization is nearing a catastrophic crisis." He nodded toward the side wall chart with its multi-colored lines. "There's the course of history as far back as we know it. Civilizations arose and fell. But we've learned something — their crises were predictable from various indications. We have charted these indications and know we are approaching such a crisis. Our work indicates it will be of such a nature that it could leave nothing upon which to build a new civilization."

Movius thought of the stirrings and rumblings in the Warrens, of the old people and their warnings of terrible omens. He multiplied what he had seen by the world's LP population, the reports of his own Sep couriers. This brought another thought: strange that O'Brien had not asked about the Sep movement. The indications were that he still had his spy in the Seps. Navvy hadn't reported success in his search. Could it be Navvy? He thought about this, returned to O'Brien's warning. He said, "The crisis would leave no one alive?"

"Certainly there would be people left alive." O'Brien's tone said it was a foolish question. "The whole population never participates in a revolution."

"Civilizations aren't built by charts on walls," said Movius. "People build civilizations."

O'Brien frowned. "But what kind of a civilization? One that would not profit from our mistakes, from our lessons. We seek to raise humanity above its past heights."

A story from one of his father's books came back to Movius. A Greek mythological hero, Antaeus, had gained his strength from touching the earth. He said, "You fancy yourself as Hercules and the people as Antaeus. You should remember what happened to Antaeus when he stayed too long from his source of strength."

The classical reference brought a sharp look of questioning from O'Brien. "You are a philosopher."

"A civilization without your kind of people might take a new and better course," said Movius.

O'Brien's eyes narrowed to slits; he sat back, lowered his chin.

Movius looked past O'Brien to the other chart, noted the single red line moving upward to the right. Without being told, he suddenly realized that single line had something to do with his life. It was a flash of prescience. With the thought, he knew he must not let O'Brien suspect the chart's secret was known. Movius pushed himself up from the chair. I'm important to him in some way, he thought. But what way? It's not as a spy. That's a cover for something else. And Grace is important to him, too. How?

"You have your information," said Movius. "Next time contact me in a more conventional manner. Otherwise I might not be as cooperative." He strode around the table, stopped beside O'Brien. "Have a car ready for me downstairs." The mood of perversity returned. "My wife will be worried. I don't want her worrying too much . . . in her condition."

O'Brien took three deep breaths. "See that you keep your reports complete and accurate." His voice exposed a mood of petulance quickly masked. "We need the information to predict the exact moment of crisis."

"Don't you know already?"

"We think it will coincide with The Coor's Fall poll."

Movius smiled. "Ah, the big holiday when all we have to do is bind our chains more tightly."

"We're almost certain of it," said O'Brien.

"And I'm part of your omnipotence," said Movius.

A cold smile touched O'Brien's lips. "That is correct."

"Who's spying on me?" asked Movius.

"You'd never in a million years guess."

Movius shrugged.

"We'll contact you," said O'Brien, "the next time we need some information."

"You're so thoughtful," said Movius.

Chapter 16

Grace was pacing the floor when he arrived. "Where have you been?" she demanded. "I've been frantic!"

Her worry seemed natural, but there was a false note in it somewhere, as though she were worried about something else. He said, "Sit down."

She went to a chair by the window, sank into it. Movius took a chair opposite her.

Was Grace the spy? It would be logical. But then again . . .

He leaned forward, told her about the visit with O'Brien, omitting the barb with which he had stung the Bu-Psych chief.

Grace clenched her hands tightly in her lap. "He's a cruel and callous man."

"You've met him?"

She chewed her lower lip. "I've heard about him."

The pause before she spoke, her nervousness. She was obviously lying. Movius said, "O'Brien thinks . . ."

The phone in the hall rang once. Grace jumped to her feet, ran to the phone. "Hello."

Movius turned, watched her, saw Grace glance his direction.

"I can't," she said. "It's impossible." She listened. "Why, that's not true! It's just not true! We haven't . . ." Again she listened. "I don't know why . . . I told you I can't do it and that's final!" She slammed the phone into its cradle, strode back to her chair, sat down. Her lips were compressed and she was shivering.

"Who was that?"

She glanced at him, suddenly turned to face him with that stare he found so uncomfortable. "That was my father."

Something had upset old Quilliam. Movius said, "What did he want?"

"To see me." Her eyes remained unwavering.

"Why did he want to see you?"

"He's heard I was pregnant."

A sharply indrawn breath was Movius' first reaction. He exhaled slowly, a stillness coming over him. It was less than an hour since he'd shocked O'Brien with that claim. London! The old man was the spy! He was the kind—a calculating one like O'Brien. All logic and no human feelings. A man with no instincts to trust. He'd pushed them so far under. The pattern began to take shape. Movius looked at Grace. She had pulled back into her chair, was avoiding his eyes. Movius felt a wave of pity for Grace. She was the spy in his house, but he couldn't find it in him to criticize her for it. Her tears and unhappiness showed clearly how her sympathies were torn. The pity became hate for Quilliam London. Imagine a father using his own daughter as a common pawn in such a game! The cold brutality of it left him numb.

"What are you thinking?" asked Grace.

Every mannerism betrayed her. She was in love with the man she was committed to betray. Again Movius felt the pity for her. He gave a short, mirthless laugh, stood up, went into the bedroom. The city was a dull glow of lights beyond the terrace.

Grace followed him, turned on the bedroom lights.

So it was Grace, he thought. And Navvy, too. The whole damned family! He said, "Dress in the bathroom. I'll turn my back while you get in bed."

She went to the closet, pulled out a nightgown. "Our things came while you were out. There were some extras with a card from Mr. Gerard."

"He's taking very good care of us," said Movius. "We're so valuable to him." He couldn't mask the bitterness in his voice.

She remained silent, went into the bathroom.

Movius slipped out of his clothes and into bed, turned his face to the wall. Such a strange relationship they had. He wondered if he shouldn't end it immediately, discarded that idea, telling himself it was because such a move would reveal his knowledge. He heard the door open, waited for Grace to get into bed. Her voice startled him, coming from right above him. "Dan, I'm frightened."

He turned over, saw her standing beside his bed in a thin nightgown, the almost girlish curves outlined against the lights behind her.

She saw the direction of his gaze, took an involuntary step backward, then shrugged. "We're married," she said. "I guess it doesn't really matter." She sat on the edge of his bed, looked toward the windows, hands clasped in her lap.

Movius suddenly realized she had a nice profile. *Sweet.* Her breasts were fuller than he had thought, rising and falling gently with her breathing.

"I think it was the brutality of those men who searched me." She twisted her hands in her lap. "And the way you reacted. Violence! It leaves me with a sick feeling, disgusted."

Poor Grace, he thought. She was in way over her head and couldn't see which direction to turn. So defenseless. He wanted to reach out, pat her shoulder, comfort her. The poor kid. Somehow he couldn't do it. That damned callous Quilliam! She stood up, went to her own bed, crawled under the covers, lay back. There was something elfin about her, he thought. Yes, *sweet* was the word. Sweet and elfin.

"If I could make it to be some other way, I would," he said. He reached up to the switch on the wall over his head, preparing to turn off the light. A glance at Grace showed the tears running down her cheeks. He clicked the switch, lay back in the darkness.

"You know, don't you?" she asked, her voice remote.

Had she realized her position is no longer secret? he wondered. "Know what?" he asked.

"That I love you." The voice so small, so faint.

His feeling was consternation. He didn't know what to say, waited, feeling like a coward and a fool.

"I understand how it is," she said. "I'll hold to our bargain. You can have me any way you want, Dan."

"Thanks," he said and could have bitten off his tongue the instant he'd spoken. Sure, thanks for giving me your life, everything you have. Thanks for being so brave in the giving. Sorry it leaves you so poor, old thing. Can't be helped, I guess.

A dry sob came from Grace's direction.

This could be even more complex, he thought. She loves me, yet she has to report to her father, who reports to O'Brien. So she offers herself to me to make it up, to ease her conscious. But that was too complicated; that was O'Brien's type of thinking.

"I don't know what to say," he said.

"I understand. I know you don't love me."

"I don't know how I feel. I thought all I had room for was hate. I guess I'm still numb inside."

He was surprised to find this was true.

Through the silence he could hear her uneven breathing. Suddenly, he realized how it must be for a woman like her—something tossed about by the cold logic of men. He remembered that Quilliam London knew she was supposed to be pregnant. And the old man's first thought had not been of his daughter's welfare. No. It had been about his precious plans. What made men like Quilliam London? Maybe it was fighting a system they hated and always losing. Or, never quite winning.

"Dan."

"Yes?"

"I'm sorry I've complicated your life like this." Her voice had a little catch in it.

Damn it! She was so absolutely defenseless. He slipped out of bed, was half way across to her before he realized he was nude. In the darkness, what's the difference? he thought. He knelt beside her bed, reached out, stroked her forehead. "Don't be sorry, Grace."

No, *don't be sorry, Grace.* Just listen to this one befuddled male trying to make it up to you for the cruelty of other men.

She caught his hand, pressed it against her cheek.

"No man is ever sorry when a woman loves him," he said. "Especially . . ." he paused. The lie came quite easily, easier than he had expected. " . . .when he's in love with that woman."

Her arms were about his neck, pulling him to her. He found her lips, tasted the salt tears and the gladness. She disengaged one hand, pulled back the blankets, urged him in beside her.

It was like nothing he had ever before experienced. Such a free giving, a happiness. No demanding or taking. Afterward, he went to sleep with his head on her arm, her hand stroking his hair, her voice whispering, "My darling . . . my darling . . . my darling . . ."

Just before he fell asleep the thought came creeping up out of his unconscious. "You knew love would be like this." He pushed the thought away.

Chapter 17

O'Brien paced his office, pausing occasionally to glare fiercely at Quilliam London, who sat in his accustomed chair at the end of the table, leaning forward to rest his arms upon the wood surface. On a chair beside London were an LP infirmary bag, a dark wig, rubber cheek distenders — his disguise.

The Bu-Psych chief had a feline look as he paced. "And she still refuses to come to you?"

"That's right. Three days now." London's voice sounded tired.

"Doesn't she realize nothing is more important than getting safely past this crisis?" O'Brien paused in his restless pacing, turned toward London. "What about the Sep organization?"

"I still get some reports," said London. "The man is a whirlwind. He has a second sight for picking lieutenants who will know exactly what to do." He drew in a deep breath, exhaled in a sigh. "Grace is the big flaw."

"We didn't plan on this." O'Brien resumed his pacing. "Better alert Navvy to do the job if necessary."

"I've already told him."

"What's *his* reaction?"

"He wants to know if we're certain Grace loves Movius. And he's tired of this hiding and slinking about. He's as tired of it as I am."

"You've done it before," said O'Brien. Back and forth, pacing.

"But I was younger. Walking like a young man comes hard for me." He tipped his craggy brows down. "Well, *is* he in love with her?"

O'Brien stopped. "Of course he is. The hypno-examination only confirmed what I already knew. He's in love with her, but he can't admit it to himself because he's consumed by his drive for revenge. There's a mother image underneath which fits Grace too closely. We should have thought of that."

"He's still useful to us," said London. "The organization he has accomplished is phenomenal."

"He's useful as long as he's dominated by hate," said O'Brien. "This is no time for love. If he recognized how he feels about Grace we'd have to get rid of him. He'd turn soft, cautious." O'Brien turned his back on London. "Do you think she's really pregnant?"

He could not see London shrug, but he sensed it.

"If she's not, why would Movius say such a thing?" asked O'Brien.

London stared at O'Brien's back. "To see your reaction."

O'Brien whirled. "That man is dangerous!"

"I see he got a reaction," said London.

"Of course he got a reaction!"

"I'm more certain than ever that it's not true."

"Why?"

"We've made a dangerous error. We've underestimated our man. He was feeling for a reaction, hoping to panic us into an ill-considered move."

"Such as?"

"My call to Grace immediately after you called me."

O'Brien sank into his chair. "If Grace told me what

you wanted, he has put two and two together."

"One and one together," said London. "Us."

"Tell Navvy to get rid of him."

London shook his head. "No! He's still useful. If we can coalesce the uprising behind Movius we can still control it until we're ready to dispose of him."

"And what about Grace?"

London's shoulders sagged. "That's the chance we took." His voice sank almost to a whisper. "Anyone is expendable." The hunter's eyes looked up at the chart of civilizations. "That's what counts, preserving the knowledge of that for the next civilization, showing the new ones how to ride over a crisis."

"We may have to lure Grace away from him when the time comes," said O'Brien.

London unbent, rising out of his chair like some tall insect. "I will take care of that. I still know how to handle Grace."

CR-14 was on the fifty-ninth floor of the Bu-Trans Building. The office looked out over the high-walled rear parking area where the big vans were kept, row on row of them far down below, angled precisely between white lines. By eleven o'clock most of the vans would be out working. It was early yet, though, and few had been dispatched. Movius stood at the window, looking down, waiting for Rafe Newton to appear. The cold-eyed receptionist had said Newton would be in shortly. It was a good thing. Another day of this waiting and he'd have discarded caution, started some action. But that was what they wanted him to do, obviously.

Three days they'd kept him waiting.

"Mr. Newton is out of town," the receptionist had said the first day, and the next day, and the next.

And Gerard: "Be patient. They're worried. They

want time to see if you're going to make the first move. They'll be tracing back on you, too."

Three blasted days of cooling his heels. Grace was feeling the tension of it as badly as he was. And Old Quilliam calling her every day like that, demanding to see her. Nothing to do but sit in the apartment and read, worry about him.

Movius glanced at his watch, turned around. It was a large room — CR-14 — perhaps forty feet wide and sixty long. The left wall was taken up by doorless offices separated by low, frosted glass partitions. Along the opposite wall was a row of maps on movable stands. One map had been pulled into the room. It was dotted with colored pins. Almost precisely in the center of the room was a long dark wood table, chairs around it at odd angles as though a conference had just ended. They'd been that way for three days now while people wandered in and out of the room, not speaking, not appearing to notice Movius.

Three men and a woman entered. The woman was the only familiar one, a large, squarish figure with face to match. She reminded Movius of someone. He'd been trying to remember who and had meant to ask Gerard who she was. The men were all of a type — muscular with looks so average they would be difficult to separate or remember. They had dangerous eyes which searched but seemed never to find. The woman and one man went into one of the cubbyhole offices. The other two men pulled out a map and stood looking at it, talking in low voices. They ignored Movius.

A medium height, red-haired man walked into the room. He had a wolfish, narrow-jawed look, evasive eyes which flitted across Movius without seeming to notice him.

Frank Herbert

Red hair, thought Movius. That will be Newton. He examined the man as Newton went to the two men by the map. So this was the man who had ordered Gerard's first investigator thrown down a light well. Movius touched the gun at his lapel.

The red-haired man turned away from the map, came up to Movius. "Are you Movius?" A colorless voice. The narrow-set eyes stared at Movius' lapel.

You shifty-eyed low-opp, thought Movius. *You know who I am.* He said, "That's right."

"I'm Newton." The eyes came up, flicked over Movius' face, back to the lapel. "I run this department. I'll explain your duties later." He hooked a thumb over his shoulder toward a cubbyhole near the end. "Your office is number five. Somebody should've told you."

Movius felt tension rising in the room.

Newton took his arm. "Here, I'll show you the place and where things are." He steered Movius across the room.

Yes, there was tension in the room. The two at the map had stopped talking. Movius glanced back. They had turned and were watching his progress toward the little office. Movius felt every sense in his body come alive. This was a trap! They had decided to get rid of him quickly. A compartment. What kind of a trap?

"In here." Newton was urging him to go ahead.

Movius pulled back, brushed his hand over the bulge of the gun in his lapel holster. "You first, Mr. Newton."

Tension in the room was electric. Movius flashed his left hand down to Newton's elbow and, using upward leverage, thrust the red-haired man into the office. Newton's scream was cut off by a stuttering sound, the shattering of glass. Movius slapped his lapel and the

132

tiny gun dropped into his hand. He waved the muzzle across the two by the map and the man and woman who had come out of the end office. The four were in various stages of thrusting hands into pockets.

"Bring your hands out empty," said Movius.

The hands come out of the pockets empty.

"Over against the wall." He motioned with the gun. Their faces showed shock and fright. "Face the wall and lean against it with your hands." He knew he did not need to look into the office. Rafe Newton had the reputation for laying excellent traps.

The four had eleven guns and an evil-looking dart projector designed from a stylus. After he had disarmed them, Movius ordered them to a position near the window, backed up to his cubbyhole. He glanced inside. Newton was sprawled on the floor in a spreading pool of blood. Atop a filing cabinet beside the door was a black box with a stutter gun fastened to it. Electric eye trigger. He had heard of them. Movius turned back to the four he had disarmed.

"All right. Walk ahead of me. Go slowly; don't make any quick movements. We're going upstairs."

Warren Gerard stared at the four Movius had lined up against the office wall. "They were to be witnesses to your dreadful accident, eh?" He leaned forward, peered at each one. They fidgeted. "You're somewhat of a problem."

The woman cleared her throat, glanced sideways at the three men with her. "Make us an offer."

Gerard leaned back. "Oh? You're for sale?" He turned to Movius. "See anything you'd like to buy?"

"I've been thinking," said Movius. "Say we call in Bu-Con and explain that there has been an accident. We show them Newton's prints on the trap gun." He looked at the woman. "They *are* on the trap gun, aren't they?"

"On the electric eye box. He was going to get rid of the box, leave the gun on the floor with your prints on it. An accident with a gun."

"On the box," said Movius. "That's even better. We'll say he must've been setting a trap for somebody. We've no idea who."

"What's in it for us?" asked the woman.

The anger flared in Movius. That had been a close one down there. Too close. "There's immunity from falling seventy-one floors to the courtyard!" he barked, glaring at her.

"You don't give us any choice," said one of the men.

"Nobody's giving *you* a choice," said Movius. "Just her."

"But . . ."

"Shut up!" Movius turned to Gerard, who was grinning broadly, a cold, sadistic grin. "Do you have anyone who could look after these three? I'll have to go down with what's-her-name here to see if the job's done right."

Gerard pulled a gun from a drawer. "I've still some I can trust. Go ahead."

Addington sent six men from Bu-Con. Movius had never seen them before, but they knew him, called him by name. They took photographs, measured, dusted for fingerprints, listened to the woman's story.

"Who was Newton laying the trap for?" A sharp glance at Movius.

She shrugged. "Your guess is as good as mine."

"The fingerprints check." The Bu-Con man studied the woman. "Tell us what happened in your own words."

The story came out of her mouth with a pat sureness, as though it had been rehearsed. She was merely substituting Newton's name for Movius.

They took her name. "Tyle Cotton." And that caused Movius to stare. *The cook's sister*, he thought. Now he saw the resemblance. She reminded him of the big, ungainly Marie Cotton. And Gerard's ex-mistress. Bulb-head hadn't batted an eye while looking at her, not shown by any sign that he knew her. A cold fish, Gerard.

"Mr. Movius, would you care to come over to Bu-Con and give your statement?"

He almost laughed. "Yes, I'd care. I'd care so much that I'm not going to do it."

The Bu-Con men tensed.

"If you want out of this building alive you'll just go quietly," said Movius. "You know who he was setting the trap gun for. It backfired when he got careless."

The investigator made a short note on a pad, waved his men out of the room, followed them. Presently, three men arrived with a stretcher, carted away what was left of Newton. Movius remained in the office with Tyle Cotton.

"What did they pay you for this?" asked Movius.

She turned a calculating look on him. "Promises."

"What kind of promises?" The answer had surprised him; he'd figured she was the kind to work for revenge.

"Two ranks up and all that goes with it."

He looked at the SIX above her lapel number. "When were you going to collect?"

She looked upward, her face going hard. "When Gerard was low-opped."

"He's not going to be," said Movius.

"Oh?"

"Never accept promises as payment," said Movius. "Take what you can get in your hands." He turned. "Come along."

Back in Gerard's office, Movius waved her to a chair. Gerard was standing by an open window, looking down. He closed the window, turned. Just before he closed the window, Movius had heard the faint sound of sirens. With a sick feeling, he had the sudden sure knowledge of what could be seen far down on the paving beneath the window. Three men. He shivered.

"What now?" asked Gerard. Again he gave no sign he had ever seen Tyle Cotton before.

Movius went around the desk, pulled the green pad from a drawer. This was the one, DISTRICT HOUSING— SPECIAL ORDER stamped in the corner. He filled out a fourth rank housing order for Tyle Cotton, forged Gerard's name to it, tore the order off the pad. He held it toward the woman, but did not release it.

"What's the price?" she asked, eyeing the order.

"A list of names."

She glanced toward the window. She knew what was down in the parking area, too.

Gerard found a white notepad and stylus, pushed them across the desk, not looking at her.

What's he thinking? Movius wondered.

Tyle Cotton hitched her chair forward, began writing. Movius put the housing order beside the notepad. It was a long list. She finished, took up the housing order.

"You can go now," said Movius. "Report back in the morning." He watched until the door closed behind her.

"Do you trust her?" asked Gerard. He picked up the

list, began reading the names silently, his lips moving.

"You trusted her," said Movius.

Gerard's bald head snapped up. "News travels."

"So it does." Movius looked at the list. "There isn't any need to trust her."

Gerard tapped the list with a fingernail. "Do you think this is accurate?"

"It doesn't have to be. I wanted her handwriting."

"Why?" Gerard scratched at his chin with a corner of the paper. "I could have given you that."

Movius thrust his hands into his pockets. "We have two alternatives. Either she'll go directly to Addington, tell him she's given us a false list, or she'll collect on that apartment, this being a true list of Newton's friends or a list of her enemies."

"Then what?"

"Let's have the list," said Movius. "I'm going to check it. Then I'm going to post it or one in a duplicate of that handwriting on the door of CR-14."

"Post it on . . ."

"Just post it. No threat, nothing but the names."

"And then?"

"Wait for the missing faces. When they're out three days we turn them in for evading work order."

"Addington will give them asylum."

"Certainly he will. But then we'll be able to pop off these low-opps legally and with a clear conscious."

Gerard pulled out his chair, sat down. There was perspiration on his bald head. "I think you frighten me, Movius. You work too fast."

Movius frowned. "Frighten you? I'm doing this for you to *keep* you from being frightened."

The way Gerard's bald head nodded, Movius could read his thoughts: "Daniel Movius—high loyalty index . . .

Daniel Movius—high loyalty index." Gerard's expression was gloating.

Movius suddenly thought of three men falling seventy-one stories to the paving and, with a sick feeling, realized he had put the thought in Gerard's head. *Dream on, Gerard,* he thought. *The new Daniel Movius is loyal only to Daniel Movius.*

Chapter 18

Movius was tired when he reached the apartment, his nerves frayed out by the day. He nodded to the door guards, went up in the elevator. The apartment was empty. Movius sensed it the minute he closed the door. Damn it! Grace wasn't supposed to go out! A note was pinned to the bedroom door. "Dan: I've gone with Navvy to see friends." No signature.

Friends? Sep business? He could think of nothing she was supposed to do. The organization was running smoothly, the way a good organization should. It hardly required his attention anymore.

The door chimes rang. Movius went to the door, hesitated, palmed the little gun before opening the door wide. It was Janus Peterson, the fat Bu-Trans driver Movius had appointed one of his chief lieutenants. Peterson ducked inside, waited for the door to be closed.

"Can we talk here?" Peterson's husky voice rumbled in the effort to keep it low.

"You are now conversant with a privilege of Upper Rank," said Movius. "A master scrambler on the building. It prevents any kind of tapping."

Peterson's eyes blinked. "A courier came in from Madrid today."

Something occurred to Movius. "How'd you get in

here? Nobody's allowed in this building without a permit and the place is crawling with guards."

Peterson grinned, pulled out a thin leather folder. "What kind of a permit do you need?" He pulled out a building maintenance permit signed with Warren Gerard's unmistakable scrawl. "Traced the signature from a regular Bu-Trans order."

"Anybody could do that," said Movius.

"Anybody with enough brass," said Peterson.

"Well, come in and sit down." Movius waited for Peterson to crowd his barrel-shape into a chair, then perched on the arm of a chair opposite. "What's the word?"

"People are all ready to revolt. Capetown was set to go it on their own. Now they say they'll wait for the word from here. They like the idea of all moving at once."

"How many are ready?"

"Maybe one hundred cities—the big ones. More coming in every day."

"How're we coming on the new headquarters?"

"Furniture goes in today," said Peterson. "It'll be ready by tomorrow night."

Movius nodded. "All right. Here's a message for you to take to Phil Henry: get the parts for the beam trap into a shipment to Bu-Psych by tomorrow morning. Have the men start assembling it tomorrow night. Got that?"

Peterson nodded. "I'm still not sure what that thing will do."

"It'll cause the biggest furor this government has ever seen," said Movius. "The Coor is like Montcalm ignoring the Cliffs of Abraham."

"What's that?"

"That's out of a history book," said Movius. "A general once lost an ancient city called Quebec because he thought there was one way the enemy could not reach him and failed to guard that way."

"Oh."

"The Coor and all of his advisors believe it's impossible to trap a communications beam without jamming it so that the effort would be noticeable. Phil Henry and I figured out a way to do it way back when we were in Comp Section together. Only we didn't think there was any use for the idea and dropped it."

"I'll see that Phil gets the word today," said Janus. "Soon's I can."

Movius got to his feet. "How many new recruits?"

Peterson wiped perspiration from his face with a soiled handkerchief. "Over two hundred today. That makes it sixty thousand in this city alone."

"That's a lot of people to trust."

Peterson shook his head. "It isn't hard to trust angry people. And it's not hard to find out who's angry and why. The Madrid courier said all of the people he talked to like the way you're operating. They listened close to your recordings. He said they like the way you're putting it over on the High-Opps."

The door rattled, opened. Grace stood in the doorway with a package in her arms. She looked at Peterson questioningly.

"I was just going," said Peterson.

"No need to leave on my account, Janus," said Grace.

"Have to be getting back," said Peterson. He lifted his bulk out of the chair, went to the door, turned sideways to go past Grace. Movius noted amusedly that Peterson was no thinner that way than across the beam.

Grace closed the door, dropped her package on the hall table, met him halfway across the room. They clung to each other for a moment without speaking. Grace pushed away.

Movius said, "Janus and I . . ."

"Will it wait?" She smoothed a non-existent wrinkle from his lapel, turned away from him. "You must stay away from my father. Don't let my father or Navvy get near you."

"But your note said you'd gone with Navvy to . . ."

"I made him drop me off downstairs in the basement driveway."

"Why?" he asked. "Because your father is spying on me for O'Brien?"

She whirled on him. "Don't be an oaf! I knew the second I told you about my father's phone call the other night that you'd planted the story with O'Brien." She twisted her hands. "You're going to hate me."

"I couldn't do that." Why did the lie come so easily? "I'm in love with you." Somewhere in his mind a tiny thought said, "That's right. You *are* in love with her." He'd known it for three days now — three days and nights.

"You shouldn't have gone out," he said. "It's dangerous."

"I thought I'd be back before you got home and . . ."

"And what?" He moved to her, stroked her hair.

"I had to find out what they're planning," she said. She leaned against him, her cheek against his chin. "I had Navvy take me to father's apartment to get some things I'd left there. I got away from Navvy and looked in a special place. I found a note for Navvy. It said, 'We'll have to do without.' And . . ."

"What does that mean?"

"It means they plan to kill you." She began to cry.

He held her away, looked at her. "How do you know?"

The tears rolled down her cheeks. "Because he was going to send me that message once."

Movius jerked away from her. "Until you became untrustworthy!"

She nodded.

"That's why they let you marry me. They wanted a scorpion in my bedroom. A trained scorpion that'd sting me when they gave the word."

Again she nodded. The tears were now a steady pulse out of her eyes.

The agony in Grace's expression came through the numbness in him. *She risked me hating her*, he thought. *She risked it rather than let me be killed.* He pulled her to him, stroked her head.

"I knew he was cold," he said, "but . . ."

She pulled her head back, looked up at him. "He's not really. He just can't feel anything but the need for revenge. He wants to strike back for what they did to my mother."

"No revenge is worth that."

She stared at him. "Not even *your* revenge?"

"No, not even mine." He took her arm. "Come in here and sit down. I want you to tell me their whole plan, why they called on me. Everything you know."

She held back. "First I have to know something."

"What?"

"These nights . . . have you . . ."

He looked at her, loving the little-girl expression of hesitancy. "I started to make love to you out of pity, but . . ."

"But?" The hurt showed near the surface of her eyes.

"But somewhere along the way I found you had more pity than I have." He shook his head. "Men aren't very good at this sort of thing. We try to do everything by logic and lose touch with our own feelings."

"Dan." Her face glowed. "Let's apply for sparse area resettlement. We could go away and . . ."

"Grace!"

The glow left her face.

"You know better than that, Grace. We're riding the tiger now. We can't get off the tiger until we tame it."

Chapter 19

"The ruthless side was certain to come out," said O'Brien. He stood by the window of his office, looking out at the river. "Newton was a threat. Ergo: stamp on Newton. Those other three were a threat. Ergo: dump them out a window." O'Brien turned and looked at Quilliam London where the angular man stood looking at Movius' chart.

"I see his decision index still goes up."

O'Brien crossed to his side. "Up and up. The logical brilliance of the man is uncanny."

"He once told me he doesn't use logic," said London. "The right answer just occurs to him."

"You told me."

"So I did. Up he goes. I take it this line contains the decisions of the past few days, including the one which may have smoked out our relationship."

"Yes."

"Either way the decision index must go up," said London. "If he actually has seduced my daughter and made her pregnant, that was an excellent tactical move. If it was fabrication, it shows tremendous insight."

"You talk about it coldly enough," said O'Brien.

"I shall take a great deal of pleasure in pulling the trigger myself," said London.

"Unless you happen to fall out a window first."

London nodded his angular grey head, the hunter eyes going speculative. "You were going to bring me up to date. This running around in disguise has its drawbacks. I seldom know what's really going on until I get up here with you."

O'Brien returned to his chair across the table, sat down. "Movius got Janus Peterson to ferret out the names of Newton's crowd in Bu-Trans. The list didn't coincide with one the late Tyle Cotton gave him and . . ."

"The *late* Tyle Cotton? In Roper's name, what happened to her? Did she go out a window, too?"

"Sorry, I keep forgetting you're out of touch with things."

"That is an understatement."

"Hmmmm." O'Brien pursed his lips. "Tyle tried to buy her way out of Bu-Trans and into Bu-Con with a fake list of Newton's friends. She was way out of her depth. Movius anticipated her, took the list Janus gave him and copied it in her handwriting. He posted that list on the door of CR-14. Eighty-one Bu-Trans employees failed to show for work and Tyle's body was found floating in the river."

London eased himself into a chair. "Does her sister know yet?"

O'Brien tipped his head to one side while he tugged at an ear lobe. "I told Marie. All she'd say was that it was long overdue."

"No love lost there."

"None at all, evidently."

"How did Janus get that list?"

"I gave it to him."

"And the eight-one on the list?"

O'Brien shrugged. "They'll be reported as evading work order."

"They're probably already working in Bu-Con."

"Certainly." O'Brien shook his head. "But look at the beauty of the way Movius operates."

London assumed a sour expression. "How much of this deviousness is aimed at us? What's he doing today?"

"He's out with Janus. I don't quite get the significance of it. Janus called in shortly before you arrived. Movius has been picking up electronics techs, talking with them in the rear of the Bu-Trans van while Janus drives around. One of the men he's met is an old friend from Comp Section named Phil Henry. We don't have a single line on this Henry. An apparently insignificant person."

"Did you alert Janus to the fact he may have to knock off Movius?"

"Yes. That was really why I had him call."

London sat back in his chair, staring out from under his heavy brows at O'Brien. "You've been saving some little morsel, Nathan. I know the signs."

O'Brien smiled. "I've a report from Cecelia Lang. Glass is ready to make a deal with Gerard in return for Movius' hide. Glass is really frightened."

"What if Gerard goes along with it?" London became thoughtful, answered his own question. "That would save us the trouble, give us a martyr. Martyrs have been valuable to other revolts—Nathan Hale . . . Juarez . . . Lenin . . ."

Chapter 20

Janus Peterson sat across from Movius and Grace in their apartment. He seemed uncomfortable, kept looking out the window at the dusk settling over the city. "I had to come back and tell you. I've been thinking for two days now."

Movius sat on the arm of Grace's chair, a hand loosely across her shoulders. "What else, Janus?"

"That's most of it, Dan. I've been working for O'Brien eight years now. I guess I've always held your opinion of him—a cold-blooded fish thinking of nothing but his charts."

"He never got things really unified and moving, though," said Movius.

"Not the way you're doing. He always kept putting us off, saying the time wasn't yet, be patient."

"When did you run out of patience?"

"When he explained how I might have to pull the trigger, that he was going to get rid of you when you'd served your purpose. I started wondering if I'd wake up some day and find out I'd served *my* purpose."

"A lot of people feel that way," said Movius.

"Revolution is a mean business," said Peterson.

"Not that mean," said Grace. She looked up at Movius. "If you destroy all human values, you wind up right where you started. That's why I'm backing Dan instead of my father."

"And brother shall be turned against brother and the child against the father," said Movius.

"What's that?" asked Peterson.

"Something I heard a pastor say once."

Peterson hauled his thick bulk out of the chair. "I'll be shoving off." He grinned at Movius. "I've a little of your work that needs doing."

"Did you get the word to Phil Henry?"

"I sent a man right after I left you before."

Movius got to his feet. "Thanks for coming clean with me, Janus. Will you explain to the others that I understand how it is?"

"We knew you would," said Peterson. "We talked it over before I came back here."

"He does understand," said Grace. "That's why we need him."

Peterson gave Grace a piercing look. "Just see that *nobody*," he emphasized the word, pausing after it, "gets in here who don't belong in here." He propelled his huge body toward the door, opened it as the chimes rang.

Over Peterson's shoulder, Movius caught a glimpse of Navvy's face. Peterson suddenly thrust himself against Navvy, there was a short scuffle; Peterson pulled away, exposing Navvy, who was rubbing his wrist. "Don't try them tricks on the man who taught 'em to you," said Peterson. He pocketed a fap gun.

Navvy's face was flushed. "I came to find out."

Peterson took Navvy by the collar, hauled him inside, shut the door. "Find out what?"

"If she is." He looked at his sister. Grace was standing beside Movius.

"It's my fault," she said. "O'Brien loaned us a car

today and I let Navvy bring me in the building, the basement driveway, with it. I assumed he'd got right on out. He's been waiting to come up here instead."

Movius nodded.

"You want to find out if your sister is what?" demanded Peterson.

"Like O'Brien said."

"What did O'Brien say?"

"That she was pregnant and had gone back on us."

"O'Brien's a cold potato who needs more time in the fire," said Peterson. "Dan knows all about him and your father and about you and Grace, too!" He propelled Navvy roughly into the room. "I got a question for you, Navvy London."

Navvy didn't look at him, stared from Movius to Grace, back to Movius.

"How long you figure it'll be before your father or O'Brien tosses *you* into some hot spot that suits their high and mighty convenience?" demanded Peterson.

A pouting look came onto Navvy's face. It was unlike him and it surprised Movius.

In a stiff manner, Navvy said, "I'm ready to serve wherever I'm needed."

Peterson curled his lip. "All self-sacrifice. Now ain't that pretty?" He raised his voice to a near bellow. "And what kind of government do you think their kind'd set up? I'll tell you what kind! One where you or me wouldn't count, where everybody'd be expected to give in to the needs of whoever was running things." Peterson grabbed Navvy's shoulder, shook him. "You dumb head! What kind of a Sep do you think you are? That's the kind of government we got now!" He pushed Navvy farther into a corner.

"I never thought," said Navvy, sinking into a chair.

"Of course you never thought!" growled Peterson. "That's the trouble with us. We never thought because we believed that smart thinking could solve every-thing—somebody else's thinking."

Chapter 21

O'Brien's male secretary opened the door softly, peered in at his boss. The Bu-Psych chief stood at the table which served him as a desk, working with a circular slide rule, pausing to jot notations onto a sheet of paper. Beads of perspiration went unnoticed on his cheeks below the greying temples.

"Movius is downstairs," said the secretary.

O'Brien looked up. "Movius?" It was as though he didn't know the name. Then, "Movius!"

The secretary nodded. "His driver just let him out. He walked right in and asked to see you."

O'Brien moved around to his chair, sat down, tugged at his ear. "Well, send him up then." He managed to look surprised when the secretary ushered Movius into the room. "Something special to report?"

Movius looked down at O'Brien. "No remarks about coming to you openly like this? No recriminations?"

"Who needs to know *why* you're here?"

"Perhaps Quilliam London," said Movius. He sat down across from O'Brien, enjoying the way the man glowered at him. "You rather upset Quilliam the other night. You should be more considerate." He stared at O'Brien until the latter looked away. "That's often the trouble with psychological people—so much logic that they have no human feelings."

"Why are you here?" asked O'Brien.

"For advice. My informants tell me Glass is ready to make a deal with Gerard. I'm the price."

"Your infor . . ."

"Some of them used to be your informants," said Movius. "I want to know how desperately you feel about this crisis?"

O'Brien sighed. "You really want to know, do you?" He stood up, went to the big chart. "Look at this." He pointed. "This blue line is the course of civilization. Here's the Greeks. This bump's the Romans. Back here's the Chinese. Here are the Mongols. Genghis Khan here . . . Kublai Khan on this slope. This is the Anglo-American. Over here is Motojai, pre-Unity."

"I'm familiar with the history," said Movius.

O'Brien glanced at him. "Yes, of course. Your father." He turned back to the chart. "Now follow this yellow line. It's a little faint against the white paper, but you can see that it coincides most remarkably with the rise and fall of civilization. The red line also is of interest and the brown one on top. Lines of cultural ascension. The others down at the bottom are individual surge lines."

Movius bent to peer more closely. "Individual?"

"Persons who influenced the course of history."

Movius straightened. "What is the yellow line?"

"It's a blending of many things—economic activity, sun spots, lunar influences, atmospheric electrical changes, gravitational flow, magnetronic fluctuations on the earth's surface, random impellation interpreted by charting cosmic rays . . ."

"It slopes down here," said Movius, pointing to the right. He looked back along the undulant course of the line. "Farther down than it's ever been before. Is that the present crisis?"

"Yes. Something special in the way of crises. We are in the bottom of the curve now. That means conditions are ripe for an upheaval. It will only take a catalyst."

"The Fall poll."

"I believe so. Many people are bitter about the polling. Your activity has a great deal to do with this, showing people how the Selector is by-passed, how the questions forecast the answers, how the whole thing is maneuvered. When they are asked to participate again in that day-long activity which they now consider farcical — that may be the push that's needed."

"How bad will the crisis be?"

"We can only guess. The mathematics and knowledge by which we made this prediction were centuries in gestation."

Movius smiled. "Now you need a midwife."

O'Brien appeared surprised, tugged at his ear, head cocked to one side. "Why, yes, I guess we do. I'd never quite thought of it in that way."

"How precious is the midwife?"

O'Brien turned away. "I've been aware for some time that we've very much underestimated you, Movius."

"No." Movius shook his head. "You've misestimated me."

"How is that?"

"Is this business important enough to see me as Coordinator?"

O'Brien whirled on him. "Are you trying to make a deal with me?"

Movius stared down at him. "No. The fact is, I've come to a decision."

"What decision?" O'Brien bristled. He looked like a

small hen demanding of a rooster where he had been until this hour.

"You want to save the world from a catastrophe which would lose this valuable knowledge." Movius pointed toward the chart. "That's a laudable ambition, although of questionable value. I want to save the world from the cold brutality of such as you."

O'Brien's eyes blazed. "Brutality! Is it brutal to . . ."

"Oh, be quiet," said Movius, his tone disgusted. "Who's to be the judge of who we might argue here? Each of us thinks he knows his motives. The truth is, we actually know very little about our motivations and probably care less. The difference between us, O'Brien, is a matter of distance—the distance from our racial roots at which we operate. You're far away; I'm close."

"Mmmmm," said O'Brien.

"And this loyalty index. I've been studying that. It really has damned little to do with loyalty."

"True," said O'Brien. "The index could be said more truthfully to measure the degree of compassion a person feels for his fellow humans. Loyalty index is a popular catch phrase tacked onto the measurement because the higher the index the greater degree of loyalty to a cause or person."

"Much of your business is a sham," said Movius. "I've decided that . . ."

"Ah, yes, the decision," O'Brien interrupted him. "When did you come to this decision, if I may ask?"

Why would he want to know that? Movius wondered. He shrugged, said, "The other night . . . in bed."

"Ahhhh." O'Brien made the sound as though he had seen a great light.

"More of your stock in trade," said Movius. "*Ahhhhh.* The witch doctor's mysterious incantation."

He raised his hand as O'Brien started to speak "I just about have you figured, O'Brien. You set me up for this business. You picked me up when I came along, way back before I was Liaitor. You decided that here was something you could use. You . . ."

"Just a moment." O'Brien sounded bored. "Why should we want you?"

"In a moment," said Movius. He turned, marched to the chart which he knew plotted some element of his life. "You want to ride the tiger, O'Brien?" Movius reached up, ripped the chart from the wall. "Then wake up to the fact that your tiger is no longer tame. Prepare yourself for some scratches."

"You will not leave here alive," said O'Brien.

Movius smiled at him. "Don't be rash, O'Brien. Find out your tiger's strength first. A wounded tiger is much more dangerous than an unwounded tiger."

"So?"

"This is a fallacy." Movius kicked the chart on the floor. "No man can be reduced to a line on a chart with any hope that predictions from that line will be infallible. You cannot know what will stimulate a man's awareness from minute to minute. The person you've charted here is many people — the son of a frustrated ex-teacher, a rising executive, a blind young man who lived in a world of his own projections, then the low-opped seeker after revenge, the focus point of a revolution."

"And now he's the great lover," said O'Brien tauntingly. "Movius, you've outlasted your usefulness."

"Is that your latest prediction?"

"Yes. Primarily, because you've become aware of your position. We needed you for the figurehead of the revolution. You were valuable as long as you were ignorant of that fact. A man conscious of his own importance to such a movement does not have the reckless courage this job requires."

"You informed me yourself, you know," said Movius. He put his hands in his pockets, watched O'Brien.

The Bu-Psych head turned away. "That was my mistake. But it isn't irreparable. There are other . . ."

Movius interrupted him with an abrupt, barking laugh. "I warned you, O'Brien, not to do anything rash. Listen carefully. I have a dozen men in your organization. They will kill you if you harm me. You have no way of . . ."

"How could you? You haven't had the time!"

"Time? What is time? Rather, say I've had the opportunity. Now I'm going to tell you my decision. I'm taking over, O'Brien. You'll listen to how you fit into *my* plans and you'll do what I say or else."

O'Brien sounded more hesitant. "Oh?"

"Today, I started a chain of events which will eventuate in by-passing the master opinion controls."

"That's impossible!"

"I'm happy to hear you say that, O'Brien. I'm hoping The Coor et al feel the same way."

"It is a known scientific fact that the control beam cannot be . . ."

"Will you shut up?" Movius glowered at the man. "Save your double talk for someone you can impress. Nine years ago in the Comp Section another fellow and I figured out a way to tap the beam. We did it as an exercise for the very reason that people said it couldn't be done. Then we dropped it because we didn't see any value in it and knew it would cause a lot of trouble for us. People would want to know why we did it."

O'Brien's mouth was open. He closed it with a snap.

"I am about to demonstrate the danger of fixed-pattern thinking. The proper moves have been right in front of your nose for so long you haven't been able to see them. You see through them."

O'Brien leaned back against his table. "Do go on." His tone was patronizing.

"The registration kiosks of the world are controlled from this city," said Movius. "The small percentage of the population which constitutes a sample is called . . ."

"If you mean that the questions are formulated here, transmitted from here and computed here, yes, that's true. But what does that have to do with . . ."

"What would happen if The Coor's transmitter fed its questions into a relay station? Let us say that relay station is equipped with a staff of about four of your best semantic analysts, who then take his carefully pre-pared question and distort it to obtain precisely the answer The Coor does not want. Then this relay station puts the new question back on the beam. Say a three minute delay."

"It couldn't be done!"

"Couldn't it? It's going to be done. I've a crew working on it right this minute."

O'Brien shrugged. "All right then. You do it. Your interference would work once—maybe twice; then Glass would stop putting questions until he'd smoked you out. And what would you have accomplished?"

"You have it figured the way I figure it," said Movius. "But you miss the essential point." He held up a hand, bent down a finger. "We wish to stage a revo-lution." Another finger bent down. "One of the gov-ernment's strongest points is the inertia—the 'Oh, what the hell?' attitude of so many people who don't feel they have cause to revolt. They're a millstone around the neck of our revolution. Potential informers, potential enemies every one." Another finger bent down. "And why? Because the government operates behind a mask of legality which they feel has the semantic label *correct.*"

"You sound like Quilliam London," muttered O'Brien.

"Do I really?" Movius bent his other finger, clenched his hand into a fist. "We take away the government's major tool of legality and they will be forced to come out from behind the mask. It's either that or admit they've loaded the questions to get their own answers. They'd never do that."

"Everybody knows that anyway," said O'Brien.

"You make a common error," said Movius. "Everybody knows this because I know. Before many people could know this they'd have to admit to themselves that they'd forged their own shackles and raised their own despots. Most people don't have a strong enough ego to do that. History has never seen such a mass admission. No. People strike out at a scapegoat, someone or something else which absorbs all of the personal guilt." Movius smiled. "I'm fitting Glass for so tight a hair coat you won't be able to tell him from a goat—a scapegoat."

O'Brien straightened. "So you're taking over. If you think your silly threat against my life is going to make me . . ."

"How would you like to have Glass, Gerard, Addington and company learn about your secret organization, your charts, your plans, your position as advisor to the Seps?"

The Bu-Psych chief paled.

"That's a much better threat, isn't it? If anything happens to me they *will* learn." He paused for effect. "You will select the expert staff I have requested. Four men. More would cause delay. Outline to this staff exactly what they will be doing. Have them ready for me at a half-hour's notice."

O'Brien seemed in a trance. "Half an hour's notice." He swallowed. "You can't . . ." He broke off, studied the look on Movius' face. "Where will they report?"

"At the new Separatist headquarters. It's under the street between here and the Bureau of Education Building. The entrance is in your sub-basement, conduit tunnel two on your plans. We're using your building air-conditioning system."

"Under my . . ."

"We're also going out with your phones through a section of your switchboard."

"But . . ."

"The Sep movement really started here, O'Brien. It's only fair that it make its big bid from here."

O'Brien sank into a chair.

"In case Gerard goes for The Coor's deal, I want asylum in Bu-Psych," said Movius.

O'Brien had trouble finding his voice. "Can't do it," he piped. "We haven't the strength to fight an open . . ."

"Then Grace and I will hide in the new headquarters."

"Grace and you . . ."

Movius glanced at his watch. "I'm due back at Gerard's office right now."

As he left the building, climbed into his car, Movius noted that it hadn't been too difficult to turn the tables on the omnipotent O'Brien.

Upstairs in Bu-Psych, O'Brien was repairing Movius' torn decision chart, replacing it on the wall.

Chapter 22

Gerard leaned back in his chair, put a hand over the mouthpiece of his phone, glanced at Movius. He looked like a small bald devil sitting behind the big desk, Movius thought. Gerard said, "It's . . ." He talked back to the phone. "Yes, I'm still waiting." He leaned forward, scribbled on a slip of paper, "It's Glass wanting to talk to me," shoved the paper across the desk.

Movius bit a hangnail off his thumb, retrieved the paper. He glanced at it, tossed it back to the desk.

"Hello," said Gerard. "Oh, hello, Helmut. Haven't heard from you since last month's conference. . . . Oh, I've been quite well, thank you. And you? . . . Good to hear it. What can I do for you? . . . Movius? Yes, I believe I have a man by that name working for me. His order came to us through the selector." Gerard smiled at Movius as he listened. "Are you sure it's the same man? You make him sound dreadful. Leader of the Seps? Goodness! Say . . . now that you remind me, wasn't he once engaged to that blonde I saw with you at the Festival? I believe I heard some story about Movius throwing her over before you met her . . ."

Movius smiled at the fierce grin on Gerard's face.

"Oh, that's the way it was," said Gerard. "I guess I had the story twisted. Well, what do you want me to do about him?" Gerard nodded, listened. "Oh, I couldn't do that, Helmut. You should see the requirements I fed into the Sorter to get him. Why, they . . . Oh, you've seen his card. Well, then you understand when I say he's a valuable man. I think this Sep business is non-sense . . . You don't say . . . Have you really?" Gerard leaned back, stared at the ceiling, the phone held loosely against his ear. His expression became thoughtful. "I'll tell you what, Helmut; let me consider it. I'll call you back and let you know my decision." He nodded. "Yes. Right away. Good opps." He replaced the phone on its hook, looked at Movius pensively.

"He wants to trade you something attractive for my hide," said Movius.

Gerard swung around to face his desk. "My own man in Addington's job."

"He's finally gotten wise to Addington," said Movius. "What does he propose to do with owl guts?"

"I can only guess. Hoist him out a window, maybe."

Movius thought of the three men Gerard had caused to be dropped from the window, fought down a shudder. He took a deep breath. "Why not ask Glass if you can put *me* in Addington's job?"

Gerard jerked his eyes up, suddenly leaned back and laughed.

The realization came to Movius that Gerard actually had not come to a decision on The Coor's offer. He said, "You know what this means, don't you?"

The laughing stopped. "What?"

"Glass is spooked."

"Because you knocked over a minor cog like Rafe Newton?" Gerard shook his head. "Even if Rafe was his nephew, don't give yourself airs on that account."

"Newton? I wasn't thinking about Newton." Movius fell silent, looked at his fingernails. What

Frank Herbert

would tempt the man? How much would Gerard believe? He believed in the loyalty index, certainly.

"You were saying," prompted Gerard.

"I've assumed you might want to be Coordinator," said Movius.

Steepled hands came up in front of Gerard's mouth, masking his expression. "What ever gave you that idea?"

Movius set his face in what he hoped was a candid, loyal expression. "I figured that if you were Coordinator and I was say in charge of Bu-Trans and Bu-Con, both of us might get a decent night's sleep."

"You what?" Gerard leaned forward, hands flat on top of his desk.

"Glass is afraid of a Sep uprising. He knows the Seps are organized as they've never been before and are all ready to move."

A crease appeared on Gerard's forehead above his nose. He passed a hand across his bald head. "He made some crazy charge about you being the leader of the Seps."

Here it is, thought Movius. He said, "That was no crazy charge. I am just that."

Gerard arose half out of his chair, sank bank. He put a hand in his pocket.

"What would happen if there was a Sep revolt in which The Coor was killed?"

In a cautious tone, Gerard asked, "The Coor, Addington and a few others?"

"That's right. One man would not be enough."

An eager note crept into Gerard's voice. "There are about fifty who would have to be eliminated."

"You know them all, of course?" asked Movius.

"I could give you a complete list, including their

habits and the easiest way to get them." Gerard's voice grew cool. "How could such a revolt be arranged and still . . ."

"They will do what I say without question," said Movius. "They were completely disorganized before I took over."

Gerard leaned forward, toyed with a stylus. "What did you plan to do?" he asked, looking at the stylus.

Movius pressed his hands against his legs to steady them. "I hadn't planned any farther ahead than killing Glass until I hooked up with you."

Gerard's eyes glittered. " Now you want to make *me* Coordinator? What's to keep you from just taking the top spot yourself if you know the way?"

Movius breathed a silent prayer to Gerard's belief in the loyalty index. "You saved my life. Besides, what do I know about the job? You've served two terms in it."

"So I have." Gerard seemed to bask in a memory, suddenly frowned. "But that was before Glass decided he could pass out the job as a payment for services."

"I propose we low-opp Glass," said Movius.

Gerard came to a decision. He reached down, jerked up the phone. "Get me Helmut Glass at Com-Burs." He waited. "Helmut, this is Warren Gerard . . .. Yes, I've decided *not* to accept. Movius is too valuable to me . . . No, I'm not holding out for more . . . Sorry, I haven't any price to name . . . I don't think that would be advisable at all, Helmut . . . Certainly I realize you're the head of the government, but you have to obey the opps just like the rest of us. Movius was legally opped to me by the Sorter. He's a legal government employee working in my department. He's . . . You're a fatuous bastard yourself, Helmut!" Gerard slammed down the phone.

Movius wondered how long Gerard had been wanting to say that to Glass. The words had been spoken with such relish. He felt a tired aching in his hands, looked down and saw he had been clenching and unclenching his fists.

Gerard breathed deeply, eyes glazed with excitement. "What do you need, Dan? You name it. Anything in the organization."

"We've a tough few days ahead of us," said Movius. "We're keyed to go the night before the Fall poll. That's four days away. The word is that Glass will put a few preliminary questions to the opp on the seven o'clock that night in preparation for the following day's heavy polling. We've a surprise waiting for him."

"What do I provide?"

"Treble the guard on the apartment until tomorrow. My wife and I are going into hiding. Set up a few scattered power failures for tonight, tomorrow and the next day, a few unexplained explosions. Give them something to investigate and worry about." Movius became thoughtful. "Bu-Trans services the relay ship. Now . . ."

"Only the movable machinery," said Gerard. "We service it, but we don't staff it except with a few technicians."

"Could something happen to just the power transmission?" asked Movius.

Gerard tapped his teeth with the tip of the stylus. "I believe so. When would you want this to happen?"

"At seven o'clock the night before the Fall poll, the moment The Coor puts his first preliminary on the beam."

"They have emergency power," said Gerard. "You want that put out, too?"

"No, just the relay. Every moving vehicle in the city

that depends on the transmitter should come to a stop. Let me have a turbo-copter for my own transportation. How many have you?"

"This is Bu-Trans," said Gerard. "We control most of the world's supply. There are about two thousand in the city here, perhaps twenty-five thousand more at sub-depots around the world."

Movius was stunned. He'd been blind! "How could we contact them?"

"Over the routing teletype," said Gerard. He bent his bald head toward Movius. "What's on your mind?"

Movius slapped a hand onto the desk. "I'm going to send five girls up here with some lists of code names. You send out the orders to people you can trust. Those copters are to be put at the disposal of the people with these code names. This revolt is going to be fought from the air."

He was almost to the new Sep headquarters before a sudden thought struck him: *What if Gerard does an about face? He'd hold the key to the whole revolt. They could pick up the district leaders one by one as the men checked in for their copters.* Well, it was too late to turn back now.

Chapter 23

"I shall kill him when he returns to his apartment tonight," said Quilliam London. He paced to the windows where the pigeons were conducting their morning watch on the streets, strode back to the table, slammed a fist down on the wood. "He's too dangerous! We'll have to get along without him."

"Don't be hasty, Quilliam." O'Brien rubbed at a greying temple. "I've been doing some re-evaluating of our records on Movius. The job he has done is little short of a miracle. In just two months he has eighteen million people so organized they're ready to die for him."

"Most of those district organizations already were in existence," said London.

"But not unified. Not unified." O'Brien lifted a sheaf of papers on the table, let them drop. "Reports, reports! You should see them. No wonder Glass was ready to make a deal with Gerard. No wonder Gerard is hypnotized by the man. Big thefts of arms. Whole warehouses. EMASI! scrawls all over. There were nine power failures in this city alone last night. They've never been this bold! Movius has inspired them and we *have* to control that unifying force!"

"High-Opp!" London's voice took on a sour bitterness. "We lost control of Movius when he walked in here and started giving you orders."

"But the diabolical cleverness of the man! Bypass the poll control, force The Coor into the open. Make him take off his mask."

"What difference does it make with a revolution under our noses?" demanded London. "This man will blunder us into an open battle before we're ready."

"But . . ."

London cut him off. "You said yourself his idea would only work twice at the most and then Glass would move to smoke him out."

"I see you miss the point," said O'Brien. He tipped his head, worked a fingernail at the corner of his eye. "My work of re-evaluation includes a study of our position relative to Movius." He found whatever it was in the corner of his eye, straightened his head. "We chose Movius for a number of reasons." O'Brien ticked them off on his fingers. "Susceptibility to our methods of, shall we say, ignition? Brilliance of intellect, high achievement, ability to make correct decisions, ambition . . ."

"Don't forget the loyalty index," said London coldly. "You know damned well he's out for number one now. And he'll be cautious. He's lost the essential boldness."

"Maybe, maybe not," said O'Brien. He studied London.

"He has you enthralled, too," said London. "Bah!"

"Perhaps we chose our figurehead with more skill than we supposed," said O'Brien. "Let's not forget that a crisis time requires strong measures and a strong hand to execute them."

"Execute!" London stamped across the room to the master chart. "He'll likely ruin everything. It's damned strange, Nate. Only last week our positions were reversed.

You were wanting him eliminated and I was saying we should wait."

"You know, I was just thinking the same thing," said O'Brien. He ran a hand through his hair. "It's odd, Quilliam, but we've never discussed one vital element of our plans. I believe we've tacitly avoided it."

London turned away from the chart. "And what would that be?"

"After the revolution, who did you plan should be Coordinator?"

The old man drew himself up. He had never looked more like an ancient hunter — knobby, austere. "Myself, of course. Who else is qualified to render dispassionate judgments?"

A look of tiredness washed over O'Brien's face. "I guess I'd anticipated that." He looked up at London. "I had thought, though, that our object was to give the government back to the people."

"When they're ready for it," said London in a clipped tone.

O'Brien smiled vaguely. "Movius would say they've always been ready for it."

London banged a fist against the master chart beside him. "Movius! Did Movius devise this? Did Movius anticipate the course of history?"

"Who *did* do these things?" O'Brien's voice was low.

"We did," said London.

"Allow me to correct you." O'Brien raised his voice. "Because of the accident of time which placed us at this point in history, and for no other reason, we are in a position to reap the benefits of five hundred years of work by thousands of others. Without their work we'd have nothing. And as far as predicting the course of history, are we sure — certain sure — that we were the force that brought Movius on stage?"

London curled his lip. "Don't turn metaphysical on me, Nate. I can forgive you anything but that. Your other argument has spoken for me. Because of all this work, we *are* in a position to save the best of one civilization for the next one. But our work and the work of those before us is being endangered by this egoistical upstart, Daniel Movius!"

O'Brien cocked his head to one side. "On what do you base this judgment?"

"On my ability to interpret the course of events and decide when the time is ripe. Movius is moving too rapidly." He shook his head. "Much too rapidly."

"You said yourself that the crisis would come at the time of the Fall poll," said O'Brien.

"I have revised my opinion."

"The revision seems to have come at the very time Movius seems in a position to win the revolt and take over the government."

London's eyes blazed. "Are you trying to say that . . ."

O'Brien stopped him with a curt wave of the hand. He stood up, the look of tiredness more pronounced. "I had hoped to avoid this, Quilliam." He brought a rolled chart from beneath the table, opened it to show that it was transparent. A single blue line slanted across it, curving up and down. The transparent chart fitted over the chart on Movius. O'Brien taped it in place. The blue line on the transparent chart showed a flatter gradient, more sharp downslopes than the red line on the chart beneath it. The difference was pronounced. The red line climbed at a steep angle. "This blue line charts the decision index of a man named Quilliam London," said O'Brien.

London's cheeks flushed; he compressed his lips,

breathed noisily through his nose. "That was an evil turn to do an old friend, Nate." His voice was low, controlled.

"I had to do it, Quilliam. If it's any consolation, I've a chart on myself here. It's about the same as yours."

"That man is dangerous," insisted London.

"He's dangerous to *us* if we threaten him," agreed O'Brien. "Only if we threaten him."

"Have you given up then?" London looked down at the little psychologist.

"Given up? No, I wouldn't call it that." O'Brien turned away from the wall. "A psychologist looks for many things in people and events. I missed a point in observing Movius, although he has not missed this point in observing himself. He has said at least once . . ."

"Bah!"

"Don't interrupt. Movius has his roots deep in the unbeatable wellspring of the collective unconscious, that living juggernaut which actually governs . . ."

"Nonsense! That is not logical!" London seemed at the end of his patience.

"That is exactly correct," said O'Brien. "Movius is not using logic. He is depending upon instinct. He is in contact with his feelings. There is an ancient colloquialism which precisely fits this situation: Movius is *flying by the seat of his pants.*"

"Of all the utter . . ." London broke off, gritted his teeth. "You're going to sit by and let him destroy everything we've planned."

O'Brien shook his head. "I've explained the significance of our work to Movius as well as I am able. I'm hoping he will use the knowledge to advantage. That would preserve it."

"You're hoping!" The old man's tone was taunting.

"You're not planning—you're *hoping!*" Suddenly, the old fierceness returned to London. "What about our plans, Nate? I ask you that!"

O'Brien shrugged. "Sometimes the best laid plans . . ." He broke off. "Someone has come along who demonstrates without question he has greater planning ability than we have. I consider it wise to turn the planning end over to him."

"In the worst crisis time in all history? Movius doesn't appreciate the first significance of a crisis!" London turned his back on O'Brien. "You've lost your spine, Nate. This isn't like you."

A note of pleading came into O'Brien's voice. "No, Quilliam. I've awakened. As I listened to Movius . . ."

"Listened to Movius! Great Gallup! For six weeks I ate, slept and drank Movius! He's nothing but a monumental ego!"

"We mustn't interfere with him," said O'Brien. "I'm convinced of it."

"Well, I'm not convinced!" London strode to the table, picked up the wig which disguised his hair, stuffed the cheek-distenders into his mouth. He picked up the infirmary bag, went to the door. "Movius is a positive threat to all of our plans. He is going to be eliminated."

"Just a moment."

The command stopped London at the door. The old man turned, the disguise making him look youthful in a bizarre way. "Yes?"

"Who will do the eliminating?"

London patted the infirmary bag. "I will." The hunter's eyes stared back at O'Brien.

"Why can't Navvy do it?"

A vague sag drew at London's shoulders. "You

know Navvy's gone over to Movius. He hypnotizes people."

O'Brien said, "Quilliam, your own children oppose you and agree with me."

"It makes no difference," said London. "I've come to my decision. We're going on without him." He slammed the door behind him.

O'Brien sat down at his table, waited almost a minute. With a wary sadness, he picked up his phone. "Security, please. Wilson? This is O'Brien. Quilliam London just left my office about a minute ago. He's disguised as an infirmary attendant. You'll know his walk. I want him followed. If he goes anywhere near Movius' apartment he is to be stopped." O'Brien hesitated. "Be careful. I believe he has a stutter gun in that infirmary bag." He listened, spoke again in a lower tone. "Yes . . . shot if necessary."

Chapter 24

It was late when Movius entered his apartment building. He saw the woman standing in the elevator. She was turned half away from him, face averted. Something vaguely familiar about her, but he was anxious to get upstairs to Grace. They had a lot of things to do if they were going to get out of the apartment tonight and into the hidden quarters beneath Bu-Psych. He punched for the fiftieth floor, stepped back as the door closed. Then he thought maybe this woman doesn't want to go that high. He turned to her, started to shape the question. It never got past his lips.

Cecelia Lang!

"Hello, Dan." She smiled, a slow, controlled movement of lips which never reached the eyes.

That soft, silky voice. It had made him shiver once. Now it filled him with a kind of dread. He found his throat was dry and had to swallow before he could speak. "Hello, Cecie."

Just like that—*hello* and *hello. What does she want?* As though in answer to his thoughts, Cecelia pushed the red EMERGENCY STOP button, said, "I want to talk to you, Dan." She moved closer, giving him the benefit of a subtle perfume. "You haven't been around to see me."

No, by Roper! he thought. He took a deep breath. "My wife and I don't get out much." He gave the words the extra barb of flatness.

"Little Grace? She wouldn't interfere if you really *wanted* to come see me." She moved closer, put an arm beneath his. He could see the cold glints in the edges of her eyes.

Little Grace? he thought. *Little* Grace! The word implied she knew Grace. But Grace had hinted at something like that. She'd said Bu-Psych had been watching him for a long time. Sure they had. Four years of tantalizing, never-give-in Cecelia Lang. The woman with the warm, soft, promising body and eyes that always said *no*. He could picture Cecelia running to O'Brien with her reports and recalled the piercing questions she'd sometimes asked. And with this knowledge came another thought: *When the time was ripe they had her vamp The Coor so he'd low-opp me!*

The anger became a raging furnace inside him. He fought to keep the damper closed. "What do you want, Cecie?" He forced the words out without any special emphasis, as though it was of no great moment to him whatever she wanted.

Cecelia slitted her eyes, muscles tensing for the barest fraction of a second. She had sensed a wrong note. "You, silly," she said. "I want you."

Movius pushed her away gently, looked her up and down. "Take off your clothes."

"What?" Her surprise was not an act.

"Take off your clothes," said Movius in a reasonable tone. "I want to see what I'm being offered."

"Dan, please!"

He mimicked her. "Dan, please!" His hand darted out, grasped the top of her suit, ripped it open.

"Dan! I'll scream!" She drew back, clutching the torn place.

"Go ahead. I doubt anybody would hear you down here in the elevator."

She backed farther away, suddenly tried to dart around him toward the controls. He caught her arm, ripped the suit farther open. She fought him, but subsided, breathing hard, when he pinned her arms behind her back. "Dan, I came to you for help. I'm in danger."

He ignored her, ripped the suit and underclothing down to her waist as she vainly twisted and writhed.

"Dan, wait! Later. I have an apartment. We can go there." She stared up at him with a kind of hungry fascination.

Movius looked down at her pink skin, remembering all the nights he had stayed awake, wondering what Cecelia's flesh would feel like. Now let the bitch taste a little of her own medicine. Somehow, it wasn't the kind of revenge he'd imagined. It was flat, unsatisfying. He picked up the thread of her gasping protests.

"You're in danger?"

"Yes; oh, yes. Terrible danger!"

How had she ever followed him? he wondered. She was so obvious.

"Yes. We have so little time." She glanced down at her exposed skin. "Later, we can . . ."

He pushed her away from him, feeling a little sick with himself. "Who's waiting there with a gun?"

She started to speak, wet her lips with her tongue. "I don't . . ."

"Don't give me any more lies!" He shouted it. "You played me like a fish on a hook. Four years you played me for that omnipotent low-opp O'Brien!"

"Dan, I . . ." She was crowded back into the corner, arms up covering her breasts.

"Make him hate everything!" he shouted. "That was

the scheme, wasn't it?" He lowered his voice. "You didn't realize you could make me hate myself." The torn coveralls were beginning to slip down over her hips. "Cover yourself."

She shook her head. "I didn't . . ."

"I said cover yourself!"

He turned, punched the button for his floor. Cecelia pulled up the bottoms of her coveralls, tried ineffectually to repair the tops. It was no use; they were too badly ripped. She tied the torn sleeves around her waist. The elevator door snicked open.

"I'm not going out there like this," she hissed.

"Then stay here." He strode out of the elevator without looking back, stopped at the door of his room, unlocked it. Cecelia slipped past him as he opened the door. He went in, slammed the door.

Grace stood in the middle of the living room, a hand to her cheek, staring at Cecelia who had stopped a few feet away. Movius walked past them as though it were the most natural thing in the world for him to come home with a woman who was nude from the waist up.

"She tried to bait me into a trap," he said. "Now we have to find out who the triggerman is." He sank into a chair, his back to them.

"Who?" asked Grace, voice over-controlled.

There was a long silence punctuated by a sob from Cecelia.

"You'd better tell us," insisted Grace.

"But you don't understand," said Cecelia. She sounded as though she were about to break into tears.

"Tell us, or I think I'll kill you myself!" said Grace.

"You're all crazy," gasped Cecelia.

"That does it," said Movius. "She's told us who."

"It's Glass," said Grace. "You've gone over to him."

Movius came out of his chair and turned in one motion. "No! It's Quilliam. Has to be."

Cecelia was backing toward the door, ignoring her semi-nudity.

"Get her some clothes," said Movius. Then to Cecelia, "You'd better tell the whole thing, Cecie." Somehow, the old familiar name sounded inappropriate for this frightened woman.

"But I thought . . ." Cecelia suddenly sat down on the floor, buried her head in her hands and began to cry.

Movius turned away, went into the kitchen and took a long time mixing a stiff drink. There was a sour, sick taste in his mouth over what he had done in the elevator. Cecelia had just been taking orders. The person he should've knocked around was that self-satisfied O'Brien or Quilliam. He took the drink back into the living room. No sign of the women. They came out of the bedroom in a moment with Cecelia in one of Grace's suits. He gave Cecelia the drink. She took it without comment, drained it without removing it from her mouth.

Grace was chewing her lower lip, a sure sign she was shaken. "It *was* my father."

Cecelia put the empty glass on a table. "I didn't know. He called my private number, said he had an urgent job for me. I was to get you out of your apartment and down to . . ."

"Just a minute." Movius stepped to the phone, called O'Brien. He told the Bu-Psych chief what had happened, waited a long minute before O'Brien sighed, said, "Dan, I was hoping to cover it up without your finding out."

"Why?" Movius bit off the word.

O'Brien's voice sounded old and tired. "Quilliam had his eyes on the post of Coordinator. It's . . ."

"You mean he'd . . ."

"It's a complicated thing," said O'Brien. "Briefly, though, it's like this: he wants the power so he can revenge himself on the ones who killed his wife. Basically, he hates the LPs, blames them for what happened. I think he's a sick man and dangerous."

"A fine time to tell me," said Movius.

"I'm sorry," said O'Brien and sounded it. "I've known Quilliam so long and seen him so often, it just never got through to me what was driving him until his own actions made it imperative."

"This is awkward," said Movius.

"You mean because of Grace?"

"Of course that's what I mean!"

"I've put a special guard around your apartment. That's the best I can do. Get Cecelia out of there some way so she isn't recognized. We need her right where she is with Glass."

"The guard may help," said Movius. "Gerard's men are like a sieve. Janus comes and goes through them at will."

"My men know how to recognize Quilliam."

"Right." Movius put the phone on its hook, returned to the living room. "Your father is out to kill me." Grace sat down in a chair, turned her face away. "O'Brien has a guard on the building which may or may not be enough. We're getting out of here tonight anyway."

"If I could just go to him," murmured Grace. "I'm sure I could explain." She spoke as though she were talking to herself.

"O'Brien says he won't listen to reason."

"I didn't know," said Cecelia. "I'm kind of out of

touch with things where I am. I've always taken orders either from Mr. O'Brien or Mr. London. He just called . . . I didn't know."

"Never mind," said Movius. "What's done is done." He thrust his hands deeply into his pockets, glared at the floor. "Cecie, I apologize. Revenge is no good; it doesn't matter whose revenge."

She gave a shaky laugh, spoke in a voice totally unlike the tones which once had been familiar. "I asked for it. You just surprised me. The Dan Movius I knew wouldn't have done that." Her voice gained strength; the silky tones reappeared. "He'd have come groveling after me." Cecelia turned to Grace, gave a flippant salute. "I think you have yourself a man, honey. Keep him occupied or I may come back on my own time." She started to leave.

"Just a minute," said Movius. "O'Brien wants you out of here without being recognized. I'll have to lead you through the conduit tunnel."

"We'll *both* lead you," said Grace.

"Never mind, dears," said Cecelia. "This won't be the first time I've crawled out the back way. I suppose it opens into the boiler room as usual."

Movius nodded.

"Thank Roper for standard construction," she said and left them, closing the door softly behind her.

Grace turned toward him. "Well?" An ominous note.

Movius avoided her eyes, went to a chair by the terrace windows.

Grace followed him. "I deserve some sort of explanation."

"I lost my temper." His voice was gruff, curt.

"That's what she said. What were you going to do,

attack her in the elevator?"

"I said I was sorry. I apologized."

Grace sat on the arm of his chair. "When you lived next door to her down the hill, did you . . ."

"Good Gallup, no!" In a lower tone: "Why do you think I lost my temper? It was all that stored up frustration."

"Oh, so you wanted to!" Petulance ruled her voice. "I suppose you've had lots of women."

Movius jerked up out of the chair, whirled on her. "I'm twenty-nine-years-old, Grace. I've been a damned fool at least once every year of my life. I happen to *love* you and that's different. Let's drop the other thing, shall we? That's the past."

Her expression softened. "I'm just being female. But Cecelia Lang makes me jealous."

"Of course she does. I was engaged to her once. You know all about the job she did on me, keeping me in cold storage for O'Brien, making her little reports."

Grace came to him, put her arms around his waist, her head against his chest. "I won't be jealous any . . ." She broke off, pushed away. "I let this petty jealousy push the other thing right out of my mind."

"Your father."

"He can be terrible when he's angry." She put her hand to a cheek. It reminded Movius of someone feeling a bruise. "He's so cold, like a god sitting in judgment."

"Pure intellect," said Movius. "It loses touch with the world sooner or later."

"I'm going to find him. I've got to." She turned away.

"No, you're not." He moved up behind her, took her shoulders.

"I am. It's the only way."

"Damn it, I won't let you!"

"You're not going to stop me!"

Movius chuckled; the chuckle became laughter. "We sound like a couple of children, darling." He turned her around, took her in his arms.

"It's just that I'm so afraid for you," she whispered.

"I'll have him picked up tomorrow," said Movius. "Then you can talk to him."

"Who'll pick him up?"

"Janus can do it if anyone can."

In the end he had to kiss her more than a dozen times before she'd agree to wait.

Chapter 25

It was always dusk in The Coor's office, a sort of refined gloom. Light was absorbed by the dark paneling, the dark rug, the thick draperies. Now the dusk inside matched that outside.

"We finally have a line on him," said Addington. He took off his thick glasses, giving his face the appearance of a slab of red meat with two holes in the top and a wide slit in the bottom. "His wife was seen going into the Bu-Psych Building today." Addington polished the glasses as he spoke, returned them to his face. Again he was the owl. "She was disguised, but one of our men — Curren — spotted her from seeing her out in the Roper Road Warren the day Movius was low-opped."

"The day Movius was what?" asked Glass, staring down from his position leaning back against his desk.

"Let's not play games among ourselves," said Addington. He found a white lozenge in a pocket, popped it into his mouth, squirmed into a more comfortable position on the leather couch.

Glass pushed himself away from the desk, pointed a finger at Addington. "Nate O'Brien! He's been talking crisis for years. Do you suppose he could be manufacturing a crisis of his own?"

"Pick him up and ask him," said Addington.

The Coor shook his head. "I'm beginning to see it.

O'Brien and Gerard together and Roper knows what other departments; but those two are doing the thinking. No wonder Gerard is so bold."

"Where does Movius fit into this?" Addington swallowed the lozenge, fumbled in his pocket for another.

"I wish I knew. I'm tempted to raid his apartment."

Addington paled. "That'd mean open war. Maybe that's what they want."

Glass showed his teeth in a superior smile. "You're afraid I'd send you against that Army Gerard keeps on the building. Well, aren't you, owl guts?"

Addington flushed. "Great Gallup! Don't you start calling me that too."

"Why didn't you pick up the Movius woman when you'd spotted her?" demanded Glass.

"They took her home by copter, same way they've been moving Movius around."

"How many men would we need to crack that apartment?" asked Glass.

Addington shook his head. "I don't know. And anyway, I don't think Movius and his wife are there anymore. Gerard threw two extra crews of guards around the building yesterday, hauled off half of them today. Bu-Trans copters made half a dozen trips from the apartment to the Bu-Psych Building. I think they're holed up with O'Brien."

"Then how many to crack Bu-Psych?"

"Helmut, don't talk foolishness. We don't know how many departments are in this. We don't know how many guards."

"Then find out!" bellowed Glass. "You be ready to move the night of the seventh. They're planning something and I've a suspicion it will be aimed at the Fall poll. Well, we're going to strike first. Bring in every man you can trust. Raid your sub-districts in other cities for men."

"But that only gives me two days. I'll need . . ."

"You've had two months! Great Gallup! You've had two years! Get moving!"

Addington hoisted himself to his feet with a grunt. He shook his head, waddled from the room.

Glass went to another door, opened it. "Cecie, I've a job for you. You remember Daniel Movius? Well, he's making trouble for the government and I want you to . . ."

Chapter 26

Movius took the elevator to the Bu-Psych sub-basement. He glanced at his watch—six-thirty. There were so many loose ends, but they couldn't be helped now. Another half hour.

The room was a contrast in crudity and efficiency. Rough concrete walls enclosed a scene of hurrying messengers, clacking typewriters, people conducting low-voiced conversations on phones. It was a space about eighty feet long, perhaps half that wide, a row of concrete pillars down the middle. Early in the city's history it had been built for printing machinery never installed. Forgotten and walled off, it had been re-discovered by a Sep in Bu-Plan.

Movius entered through the access tunnel his men had hacked out. What he saw in the room pleased him. The tall black box of a scrambler dominated one end of the room, beside it an emergency generator. A large map of the world covered the opposite wall. Red pins showed Sep organizations which were ready to attack. Yellow pins indicated danger areas. A liquid incendiary tube ran along the top of the map, ready to destroy it. Every record in the room was guarded the same way.

Along one wall was a row of desks, secretaries working at typewriters. Between pillars and walls were other desks, some occupied, some empty—district cell chiefs. In the opposite aisle, more desks—area coordinators. In a far corner, two desks and a typesetting and facsimile transceiver identical to the one in The Bureau of Communication which controlled the world's opp registration kiosks.

O'Brien and a short, chunky man stood in front of the transceiver as Movius approached. The chunky man was speaking, pointing to a square black screen above the transceiver. " . . . basic fallacy. They think there's no way to tell when a message is on the beam or what scramble pattern the message is taking. Dan's idea, when we first worked on it, was to make a device which would show us the message and its scramble pattern as a motion. He . . ."

Movius put a hand on the chunky man's shoulder. "Hello, Phil."

"Oh, hello, Dan. I was just explaining to Mr. O'Brien here . . ."

"I heard you." Movius glanced across at O'Brien. "We're as ready as we'll ever be." He walked to the corner desk, dropped into the chair.

Behind O'Brien he could see a round table with four men seated around it, three talking, one doodling on a scratch pad. They were men of different sizes and shapes, but with a stamp of sameness to them. One was constructing an intricate doodle like a maze. It was a significant doodle for the men at the table. They were the Bu-Psych semantic analysts, masters at maze-like thinking.

O'Brien went to the table, addressed the doodler. "I think we'll have some work for you pretty soon, Jim."

The man, a thin-faced individual with grey hair like a disarrayed mop, pushed away his notepad. "It's about time."

Movius looked at his watch, listened to it. "Where's Peterson? He was due back here with Grace an hour ago."

Someone came into the room at the far end. A post blocked the view. Movius shifted to one side. Navvy, and hurrying. He stopped at the desk.

"I couldn't find him," said Navvy. "I thought sure I could find him. He's not in any of his regular haunts."

"Quilliam London can be as elusive as a mosquito if he wants," said O'Brien. "He slipped right away from my men."

"This isn't good," said Movius.

O'Brien rubbed the grey spots at his temples. "He could ruin everything. He knows too much about our plans."

"I should never have let Grace go out," said Movius. He slapped the palm of his hand against the desktop in irritation. "She was just like you, Navvy, sure she could find him."

"He's a master of disguise," said Navvy. "I hate to admit it, but I could have passed him a dozen times and never recognized him. I thought I'd know his walk, but . . ." He shrugged. "Then I hoped he'd recognize me and contact me." Navvy lowered his eyes. "I . . . uh, took off my disguise a couple of times just in the hopes . . ."

In unison, both Movius and O'Brien barked, "You what?"

"I wasn't followed," said Navvy. "The bull-con isn't made who could tail me."

"That wasn't what I was thinking," said Movius. He looked at O'Brien, an unspoken question in his eyes.

O'Brien held out both hands, palms up. "She might get the same notion. After all, she's his sister. Who knows?"

Movius jumped to his feet. "Navvy, do you have any idea where . . ." From his standing position, Movius saw Janus Peterson's bulky figure come through the door, hurry toward them. He was alone.

Peterson was breathing rapidly. He came up to the desk, took a deep breath, swallowed before speaking. "Dan, I . . ."

"Where's Grace?"

"I had no idea she was going to pull a stunt like that," said Peterson.

Movius walked around the desk. "Where is she?"

"Bu-Con has her. The Coor. They took her to Com-Burs."

In a flat tone, Movius said, "She took off her disguise."

Peterson nodded. "At the festival grounds. Lots of old timers hang around there. She was hoping Quilliam would spot her. I didn't know what she was going to do. I swear." He took a gulping breath. "She went into a comfort station, came out the other side without a disguise. I didn't know what to do. I saw a young fellow on the path spot her and I knew if I went to her, I'd be tabbed. She saw this fellow the same time I did—maybe she recognized him. She started to run. Just like that they were all around her. They seemed to come up out of the ground. I faced back, watched them hustle her into a car."

Movius clenched his fists. "How do you know they went to Com-Burs?"

"I spotted a Bu-Trans truck, gave them the sign and followed the car."

"In a truck?" asked O'Brien.

"They never look at trucks," said Peterson.

"Bu-Con does," said Movius. "Are you certain you

weren't followed?"

"Not unless they came through some garbage tubes . . ." Peterson lowered his eyes. "It's my fault they got her, Dan. Give me some men and . . ."

Movius turned his back. "No." He looked across at O'Brien. "Contact Cecelia Lang."

O'Brien nodded. "Right." He left the room.

"Janus, get your guards into the tunnel, see that O'Brien's Security force is alerted. The Fall poll preliminary starts in a few minutes."

"What about Grace?" asked Navvy.

"I'm hoping the confusion will give Cecelia a chance to act." Movius compressed his lips. "We can't carry off an open attack. They'd use Grace as a shield."

O'Brien returned. "Couldn't reach Cecelia. If she sees them bring in Grace, she'll know what to do. She knows their methods of questioning."

Movius picked up a phone, punched the button which put him into a special section of the master switchboard, dialed a number, waited. "Give me Gerard, please . . . Gerard? This is Dan. Monkeyshines." He waited for Gerard to respond to the code word, said, "We're ready to move. Call in every fighting man you have. Bring them across to the Bu-Psych Building. Ferry them by copter." He put down the phone, went to the map, stared at it.

O'Brien joined him. "Quite a few danger points, Dan."

Movius nodded. "Charts and pins in a map don't tell it all. Bu-Con has been throwing its weight around. Raids on the Warrens. People disappearing. Our own rumor campaign about Bu-Con torture chambers has people raging." He turned to O'Brien. "That's the important thing to watch—the temper of the people.

Now, all we have to do is make Glass show his hand, come out from behind that front of high and mighty legality."

"If you could make him take over full control without the opps," said O'Brien.

"We'll have more recruits than we can use," said Movius.

"Delicately, Dan. He mustn't suspect what you're actually trying to do."

Movius turned, thrust his hands into his pockets. "It's one minute to seven. The preliminary starts in one minute."

Phil Henry sat down at the transceiver.

"Tap the beam," said Movius.

Henry swung a control board in front of him, flicked a switch. The screen above a transceiver gleamed silver, a pulsing purple rope stretching diagonally across it. The purple rope suddenly showed a moving white band, juggling, dancing, shimmering. Henry's fingers darted over the controls. Another purple rope came up from the bottom center of the screen, matched itself to the moving white band, contacted it. The white stopped. Immediately, the transceiver in front of Henry began to clack out a message.

Movius and O'Brien stepped forward to look over his shoulder.

"Just warming up," said Henry.

On the printer tape they could read," BXBBG . . . MORE IMPORTANT THAN YOUR OPPS. NOTHING MORE IMPORTANT THAN YOUR OPPS. NOTHING MORE IMPORTANT THAN YOUR OPPS. NOTHING MORE IMPORTANT THAN YOUR OPPS. NOTHING MORE IMPORTANT THAN YOUR OPPS. MAY THE MAJORITY RULE." The machine stopped typing, continued a low humming.

"Won't they know we've stopped the message?" asked O'Brien.

"Not a chance," said Movius. "This isn't the door they're guarding. They believe the beam can't be tapped. It's in all the manuals. *There is no way to tap a communications beam short of its terminal.*"

The transceiver clacked twice—"XX," began to chatter with its message.

Work had stopped in the room. People stood in a quarter circle around the corner looking at the activity. The four men at the table pulled note paper to a handy position. They were the star performers now.

Movius ripped the printer tape out of the machine. "They're after Bu-Trans first." He read it aloud: "Would you favor reducing the number of government employees through a merging of the Bureau of Transportation and the Bureau of Control under the direction of the Bureau of Control?" He put the tape on the table.

The doodler took up his stylus. "I hope they're all this easy. How does this sound?" He began to write as he composed. "Would you favor giving greater *police power* to the Bureau of Control by merging that Bureau with the Bureau of Transportation?"

The other three men at the table nodded.

"That'll do it," said O'Brien. He passed the revised question to Henry at the machine.

Henry clipped the question in front of him. "What code number? Theirs?"

Movius fingered the number on his lapel. "Use the first three from mine—six, six, two."

"Right." He punched out the numbers and question.

"One minute, fifteen seconds," said O'Brien. "They'll never notice the delay."

Navvy moved over beside O'Brien. "They'll try to bargain with us for Grace. What do we do then?"

Through Movius' mind ran the words from his father's book: ". . . nothing is important to a revolutionist except his cause." He felt himself trembling. He'd have to go ahead as planned. Have to! Damn them!

Again the machine began to clack. O'Brien read the tape: "Code 089." He looked at Movius. "The Coor's private number." He held up the tape. "In the event of a Separatist uprising, would you give the Coordinator unilateral powers to restore order?"

Movius got to his feet. "Let that one go."

"What?" O'Brien spoke. The four men at the table looked up at Movius.

"This is exactly what we want," said Movius. "He has played right into our hands. We want him to show his dictatorial powers." He took the tape, handed it back to Phil Henry at the transceiver. "Send it through—code and all."

"That's dangerous," said O'Brien. "Unilateral power means he can do *anything* legally to restore order. He could take the opp on this one, strike right out at us."

"Let's hope he does," said Movius. He turned to Phil Henry. "Start punching this: To All LP's—Coordinator Helmut Glass has this day by-passed the opp to make himself dictator. The numbers 089 are held by High-Opp friends of the Coordinator's and were put in the Selector in an illegal manner. The opp requires that the Coordinator must open the Selector for public inspection upon demand. This demand is hereby made." Movius put a hand on Henry's shoulder. "Signed Daniel Movius, Separatist."

"If they harm Grace," said Navvy, "I'll . . ."

"You'll do nothing," said Movius. "Glass and his friends are to be the focus of public hate. If they survive the revolt, they will have public executions."

"I thought so," said Navvy. "You're just like . . ."

"Shut up!" raged Movius. "I'd like to hang them up by the thumbs and pour acid on them! But I won't. I'll . . ."

"Sorry," said Navvy.

A Bu-Psych runner ushered Warren Gerard and his gladiator secretary into the room, pointed to Movius and his group in the corner. Gerard, his bald head glistening under the room lights, made his way across the room, nodded to O'Brien. "Hello, Nate. Didn't know you were acquainted with Dan." To Movius, "What is all this, Dan?"

"This is Sep headquarters." Movius looked at Navvy, nodded toward Gerard and bodyguard. Navvy pulled a gun from his pocket, covered the two from behind.

"Quite an organization you have here," said Gerard. He looked around with a proprietary air, caught sight of Navvy's gun.

"Don't move," said Movius.

The bodyguard made a motion as though to grab a lapel gun.

"You'd be dead before you touched it," said Movius. He extended a hand, found the gun in its lapel holster, took it. Gerard and aide had five guns between them.

Gerard's eyes blazed. "So you were going to make me the Coordinator?"

"On an island somewhere," said Movius. "You won't have a thing to worry about for the rest of your life."

"Loyalty index!" said Gerard.

"I'm returning the favor," said Movius. "I'm saving your life. You and O'Brien may be the only top officials to escape public execution."

"You're damned confident of winning!" blurted Gerard.

"I can't lose," said Movius.

Navvy snapped manacles on the men's wrists, led them over to a central pillar, manacled their arms around the pillar. He turned back. At that instant the lights flickered, came back on as the emergency generator started.

"Your men on the relay ship were late," said Movius. "It's sixteen minutes after seven." He turned to Phil Henry. Before he could speak, the transceiver began to chatter. Movius bent to read the message, felt Navvy beside him.

"Would you approve a two-rank advance for information leading to the capture of Separatist leaders Daniel Movius, Nathan O'Brien, Warren Gerard, Quilliam London, Navvy London . . ." The machine went on clacking out names, district organizers, cell leaders.

"That means they've made Grace talk," said Navvy.

"Give the word," said Movius. "The revolt is on!"

Phil Henry typed out the signal, a phrase Movius had remembered from an ancient history book.

"FIRE ONE!"

Movius turned to the ring of watchers. "You have work to do. Get on it."

They dispersed to desks, phones. Some picked up weapons, went out. A tight-wave radio transmitter was warmed up on one desk.

A dead feeling settled into Movius' stomach. *Grace . . . They'll pay! Damn them!* First the revolt. Nothing else could occupy his attention now. Still he felt the numbness inside him. He wondered if other commanders had felt this way when the battle was joined and the outcome depended on the planning that had gone before. The history books never mentioned it.

The distant roar of an explosion echoed up the conduit tunnels, created a momentary ear-clicking vacuum in the headquarters room. Movius put a green pin into the map at Tampico. Another city secured for them. The radio operator came across the room with a message, scuffing his way through scattered balls of crumpled paper. "Campobella has just capitulated in Manila," he said.

Movius looked to this watch. Two a.m. They'd been at it seven hours almost. He felt no tiredness, only a dull ache every time he thought of Grace.

O'Brien straddled a chair, his back to the table the four analysts had used. "We've done it, Dan. You should be . . ."

Janus Peterson hurried into the room, ran across to Movius. "The remnants of The Coor's force are holed up in the Bureau of Communications Building. Shall we bring the place down with explosives?"

"What was that explosion I just heard?" asked Movius.

"They were trying to blast open one of the tunnels. We've got them all knocked down and sealed off with rubble."

Movius turned away, looked at the map. *Is Grace with them?* he wondered. *Do I have the right to send men to their deaths storming the place on the chance we could save her?* He shook his head. This should be a decision for someone else.

The transceiver beside him, silent since they'd sent

the order to revolt, came to life. It clacked out a single word: "MOVIUS."

He looked at the message tape, turned to O'Brien, and at that instant saw Navvy enter the room. Navvy stepped heavily over the sleeping forms of Gerard and bodyguard where they were manacled to the pillar. A Bu-Psych medic had given them shots to knock them out when they'd started interfering by yelling curses at Movius. Navvy shifted a stutter gun from his right to his left arm, stopped at the desk and leaned against it. "North and East sections cleared. The rest is mop-up." He wiped at his face, left a stream of grime down one cheek. "A Bu-Con squad took over a Warren in Lascadou, killed every man, woman and child inside. Then they had the guts to beg for mercy. A mob tore 'em apart, literally."

Again the machine beside Movius began to chatter. "WE WILL BARGAIN WITH YOU." It was signed, "HELMUT GLASS."

Navvy joined Movius at the transceiver, looked at the message. "I told you they'd offer to trade Grace for their hides."

Movius sat down at the machine, found the RR button for Registration Reply, remembered all the times he had punched that button in the kiosks to register for opps. He typed with two fingers: "THIS IS MOVIUS. WHAT DO YOU WANT?"

The machine remained silent.

Over his shoulder, Movius said, "Nate."

O'Brien stepped forward. "Yes?"

"We've won, haven't we?"

"You know that as well as I do. No doubt about it."

The transceiver rapped out, "ARE YOU WILLING TO BARGAIN?"

Movius sighed, typed, "DELIVER GRACE UNHARMED AND I WILL GIVE YOU YOUR LIVES."

There was a longer wait this time, only the humming of the transceiver indicating the beam was open. Again the machine chattered: "WHERE ARE YOU?"

"Do they want to deliver her here?" asked Navvy.

"They may already have killed her and be fishing for information," said O'Brien. "Remember, they're desperate men."

Movius put his hands to his face, leaned against the transceiver. *Yes, they're desperate men*, he thought. There was a way to be certain of Grace's fate, but he couldn't ask anyone else to take the risk.

The machine clacked: "CALL OFF YOUR MEN OR WE WILL KILL HER IMMEDIATELY."

Over his shoulder, Movius said, "Janus, tell them to hold off the attack."

Janus ran to the door, relayed the message to a courier, returned.

"I HAVE SENT THE ORDER," typed Movius.

The transceiver came right back: "MOVIUS, WE ARE ON ONE OF THE TOP FLOORS OF BU-COMM. COME OVER AND TALK OR WE KILL HER."

"You can't do that!" exploded Peterson. "Maybe they've . . . Well, maybe they just want to get both of you to kill you."

Movius ignored him, typed, "I AM COMING."

"Janus is right," said O'Brien. "Send someone else."

"Send me," said Peterson. "I let her get caught."

Something compounded of all the hate, the ambition, the fear for Grace became a hard lump inside Movius. "I'm still the commander here!" he barked. "I give the orders!"

Navvy said, "I'm not letting you go," started to grab

his arm.

Movius slapped down the hand. "She's your sister, Navvy; my wife. I'm going. Don't try to stop me."

"Let him go," said O'Brien.

The streets were dark, strangely silent. Only in the distance could he hear the *whooshBOOM!* of rocket launchers to tell him the battle was not ended. A lackluster moon ducked in and out of clouds, showed a scattering of wrecked cars on Government Avenue, a few sprawled bodies.

Three blocks to Bu-Comm. Navvy walked silently on one side, Janus Peterson on the other. They met a Sep patrol which recognized Movius and, strangely, lined up along the sidewalk, stood at attention while he passed.

"Do they know where I'm going?" asked Movius.

"I told the runner," said Janus Peterson.

Attack squads around the Bu-Comm Building opened up to permit Movius and his companions to pass. The men stood at attention until Movius had passed. There it was—tallest building in the city with its transmission facilities and huge tower. Movius looked at the building, wondered why the men were so respectful.

As though answering his unspoken question, Peterson said, "You've given us LP's back our pride, sir. We're never going to forget that."

Movius realized the big man was crying, thought, *Janus believes I'm going to my death. Maybe I am.* He could sense the presence of many men around him, could distinguish the still outlines of bodies sprawled in the street in front of the building.

"Does someone have a hand light?" he asked.

An arm came out of the darkness beside him,

pressed a metal tube into his hand. A receding voice whispered to someone, "I gave him my light." Movius had the sudden feeling of looking into the future and knew he had seen the genesis of a story. "I gave Daniel Movius my handlight the night he climbed to the Bu-Comm tower."

Movius said, "I'll signal from the south parapet. Three flashes means come on up, they've surrendered. Two flashes means wait. One flash, a delay and another flash, attack. Give me an hour. It's a long climb."

"What about you, sir?" asked Peterson. "I wish you'd let me go. It's my fault they caught her."

Movius squeezed the man's arm. "No, it isn't. Grace brought it on herself. She did it trying to protect me from her father." He released Peterson's arm. "Good opps, men."

Out into the dark street, a dark cloud obscuring the moon. A body. He walked around it. It sound of a door opening. Someone said, "In here." Movius could discern the outline of a man holding a stutter gun, heard a voice talking on a phone. "He just came in. I'll bring him right up." The phone clicked. "Elevator's over here." A hand took his arm, guided him.

"Elevator," said Movius. "I thought there was no power."

"This is the Communications Building," said the voice. "Big emergency generators here."

Of course, he thought. *There would be.*

They remained in darkness all the way up. His escort opened the elevator door, said, "To your right. Don't use that handlight." Then, oddly, the man whispered, "Good opps, sir."

He walked down the hall, heard a door open. A voice said, "In here." Another hand came out to guide him. The door closed, lights came on. It was a stuffy room, full of tobacco smoke. Thick layers of blankets had been nailed over the windows. Movius looked around. Loren Addington sat behind a table, a fat owl, nervously chewing on something. The table held a row of stutter guns, all pointing toward the door.

"A cornered rat," thought Movius.

Helmut Glass sat on a leather couch against the right wall. A stutter gun rested in his lap. His head was swathed in bandages, his left arm in a sling. A rough night for The Coor.

The man who had pulled him into the room turned out to be vapid-face, the one who had brought Grace to Gerard's office. He carried a gun in his right hand.

"Where's Grace?" demanded Movius.

Glass stood up from the couch. He carried the stutter gun loosely in his right hand. "In good time."

"I see Grace or we don't bargain," said Movius.

Glass raised the muzzle of his gun. "I could kill you right where you stand." The Coor's eyes looked like two ball bearings, grey steel, glaring from beneath the red-stained bandage around his head.

"I came up here fully expecting that," said Movius. "My men have orders to attack if I'm not back in a specified time. If they find me dead, they'll literally tear you limb from limb."

Glass sneered. "I have a crew repairing a transmitter right now. We're going to call in outside help. After we've put down your stupid revolt, your men, as you call them, will be hunted down one by one and executed. I have unilateral powers to carry out this threat."

He doesn't know, thought Movius. He said, "We hold all but eleven of the world's major cities. The handful of your people remaining in those eleven are in no position to send help."

"That's a lie!" The Coor's face flamed.

In a calm, even tone, Movius said, "By our estimates, you had fourteen million government employees in the world, a fair proportion of whom would remain loyal to you out of fear of the LP's. We have the rest of the population."

"I've a mind to drop you where you stand," said Glass.

"Wait!" It was Addington. "He may be telling the truth, Helmut."

"What if he is?"

"Where's Grace?" asked Movius in the same even tone. "I'll trade you your lives for Grace's life."

"You planted that Lang bitch on me, didn't you?" demanded Glass.

Movius understood then that Glass and Addington did not have Grace. Cecelia had rescued Grace or Cecelia and Grace had been killed in an attempt to escape. Either way, let Glass squirm for what he had done. "Yes, I did," said Movius. "Cecie was one of my most trusted operatives."

The Coor's face contorted. He raised his gun until the muzzle was level with Movius' chest.

They'll slaughter you, thought Movius. *Those men who stood at attention for me will tear you to pieces a little bit at a time.*

A stutter gun chattered. With a remote feeling of amazement, Movius watched Glass crumple to the floor.

"Drop it!" The voice was Addington's, crazy, hysterical.

Again there was the sound of the gun, the thump of

a body falling behind Movius. Vapid-face at the door! Addington stood behind the table with the gun in his hands. He dropped it to the table, held out his hands, palms up.

"I saved your life, Movius. I give myself up to you."

Movius felt a moment of disgust so deep it sickened him. He took a deep breath. "Tell your men to lay down their arms."

"You'll protect me, Movius?"

"I'll protect you."

Chapter 27

Movius looked out at the dawn light, blue and lucid on the river, the pigeons strutting on O'Brien's window ledge. He felt drained of all emotion. Would they find her?

Janus Peterson came into the office. Movius heard, turned. Peterson saluted, a stiff motion of finger to forehead. Why did all of the damned fools insist on that stupid gesture? Even Navvy.

Peterson smiled. "We found them, sir. Miss Lang got her away and they found Quilliam. He hid 'em in the tunnels."

"Where is . . ."

"She's on her . . ."

Grace pushed past Peterson. "Here, darling." She rushed into his arms.

The little elf, he thought, stroking her hair. *The wonderful little elf!* He lifted his head, saw Cecelia Lang just outside the door. For a split instant, the shield behind her eyes dropped and he saw the lost, hopeless hurt there. Then she turned away. Quilliam London took her place, came into the room, shut the door. *Something odd about Quilliam,* he thought. A glazed look in the eyes. *A gun in his hand!* Janus was backing away from the gun. Movius stiffened.

"Now the reckoning, Mr. Movius," said Quilliam

London. His voice was tight, strange.

Grace pushed away from Movius, turned. "Father! You said . . ."

"I said many things to come to grips with this monster." He motioned with the gun. "Stand away from him."

Grace shook her head.

"I said stand away from him!"

"Listen to me," said Grace. Her voice was low, flat. "If you kill Dan I shall tell the world who did it. I'll explain about your precious charts. They'll tear you and your work to pieces. Your whole life will have been for nothing!"

London's gun hand wavered. Movius saw Peterson moving a hand slowly toward a pocket.

"Grace . . ." How old Quilliam's voice sounded. "I'm . . ."

"You'll be a forgotten nothing," she said. "I'll teach your grandchild to hate your memory."

Grandchild, thought Movius. *Great Roper! Did any man ever learn under stranger circumstances that he was to be a father?*

London said, "Grandchild?" His voice sounded querulous.

Grace strode toward him. "Give me that gun!"

He handed it to her. "Yes, Leone."

Leone was Grace's mother.

He allowed Grace to lead him from the room, following quietly.

O'Brien came in sight, strode briskly into the room, stared after Grace and her father, started to turn away and whirled back, "That's Quilliam!" he said. "He swore he'd . . ."

"It's all right," said Movius. "They're going down to

the infirmary for a sedative. Quilliam isn't feeling well." He pointed to the papers O'Brien carried. "What are those?"

O'Brien seemed to recall his mission. "Dan, we've got to do something fast. They're smashing the registration kiosks. A mob broke into Comp Section, ripped apart the Selector. It'll take a month to repair it. I've a . . ."

Movius took the papers from O'Brien, waved them. "What are these?"

"Messages." Creases appeared above O'Brien's eyebrows. "I don't understand them."

Movius smiled. "Is there really something you don't understand, Nate?"

"This is no joke, Dan!" O'Brien snatched back the papers, read from the first one. "Hail, O Movius, savior of the LPs." He shuffled the papers. "That was from Athens. This is from Peking: 'To Movius, Light of the Earth.' Here's one from New York: 'Movius, we await your orders.'"

Movius pulled the papers from O'Brien's hand, examined them.

"They were brought in by couriers," said O'Brien. "They all say they await your commands."

"Let me study them," said Movius. "Bring me any others that arrive." He took the papers to the table, sat down.

"Dan, this requires immediate action! The people are completely out of hand."

"Later," said Movius, waving a hand.

O'Brien started to protest, felt a hand on his arm. He looked up to see Peterson scowling at him. "Mr. Movius wants to be alone to think." Peterson urged him toward the door.

"But this is my . . ."

"You heard Mr. Movius!" Peterson growled the words.

O'Brien allowed himself to be led from his own office.

Chapter 28

The pendulum had swung through its full arc. What smacked of the old regime could not be tolerated. Although it was not expressed in these terms, the words smacking too much of the poll government, Movius *bowed to popular opinion.*

The ceremony was held in St. Peter's Church, Rome, beneath the dome that centuries of worship had gone to preserve. It was a ceremony which took several months to research and preparation to get all of the details correct, but correct they were, down to the smallest costume for the smallest page. Video cameras focused on the event for all the world to see.

On the island of St. Kitts in the Caribbean, three exiles also watched. They sat in a warm room, open to the sea breeze and the smell of flowers. A wide verandah shaded them from the hot sun. In the dim room there was the big, square screen, the murmurous buzzing of flies.

Warren Gerard leaned back in a rattan chair, nervously wiping perspiration from his bald head. Loren Addington sat with his back to a wall, chewed placidly on a lozenge. A door slammed somewhere in the house. He jumped, resumed his chewing.

Quilliam London, his body finally failing after the years of poor food in the Warrens, sat in a wheel chair, a crutch across his lap. As the spiritual descendant of Peter lowered the golden crown onto Emperor Movius' head, Quilliam London threw his crutch at the video screen, smashing the picture tube.

"Thank you," said Gerard. "I had nothing to throw."

"I thought it was kind of pretty," said Addington.

"You would, owl guts," said Gerard.

Across the ocean in Rome, Emperor Movius stepped back, watched the crowning of his empress. The bulge of her abdomen where she carried Movius II hardly showed at all through her royal robes.

Afterward, at the remodeled Palazzo San Lorenzo, Emperor Movius granted an audience to his chief counselor, Nathan O'Brien. The audience was in a throne room with O'Brien's short figure standing at the foot of six steps leading up to a gold throne. Emperor Movius relaxed on the throne.

"Dan, I . . ."

"Just a moment," said Emperor Movius. "We are now the Emperor, the first Emperor of the entire world."

"Yes, sir," said O'Brien.

"The proper form of address is *Your Majesty*," said Emperor Movius.

"Yes, Your Majesty," said O'Brien. "Now, if you'll . . ."

"Just a moment," said Emperor Movius. "An Emperor may grant his intimates special privileges. In our private audiences, you may call us Dan."

"Yes, Dan; I know. Now . . ."

"You knew?" Movius grinned. "Well be quiet a minute, then, and listen."

O'Brien assumed an air of suffering silence. He knew he was being paid for the years he had manipulated

Movius' life. He also knew that the role of Emperor struck Movius mostly as a joke. "Proceed," said O'Brien.

"When you run out of other things to call me you may refer to our august person as Ultimate High-Opp," said Movius. "Now to business. We are this day giving you, our chief counselor, an additional duty. Duke Navvy will assist you in this duty which carries an Earldom for yourself. We want you to take over a Department of Education. We have a long list of suggested compulsory subjects."

"Excellent," said Earl O'Brien. "And now . . ."

"We have not finished," said Emperor Movius. "We also want you to bend your efforts to a plan of oppression for our peoples."

"A what?"

"We want to be gently oppressive," said Emperor Movius. "When it has become too much for our peoples to bear, they will come to us demanding their equivalent of the Magna Carta. Protesting the divine rights of Emperors, we will grant their demands."

"So the cycle starts again," said O'Brien.

"Act," said Emperor Movius. "Lastly, we wish you to start research on space flight. There should be no lack of volunteers. A suitable refuge should be found for ourselves or descendants, anticipating the moment when the cycle rounds its next curve."

"Are you quite finished?" asked O'Brien.

"Yes." Emperor Movius gave a lordly wave of his hand. "Say, I'm getting pretty good at the high and mighty attitude." He waved the hand once more. "Notice the wrist."

"I have an important message," said O'Brien.

"Eh? Oh, yes, of course. Proceed."

O'Brien cleared his throat. "I have a report from one of our cell chiefs in Istanbul. A group of sixty-one former government employees has started a revolutionary group there. They call themselves the 'Unity' party. They . . ."

"Unity Party," said Emperor Movius. "That has a nice sound, hasn't it?"

O'Brien glared at him. "Dan, this is serious! The report is that these are some of the toughest boys from the old government and they may have friends elsewhere."

"What do you want me to do?" asked O'Brien.

"Roper's Na . . . I mean, Great Emperor! Isn't it obvious?"

Emperor Movius shook his head. "No."

"I want authorization for a control squad to check back on these people and eliminate them before they grow stronger."

Emperor Movius jumped from his throne. "You'll get nothing of the kind!" He pointed a finger down at O'Brien. "We are holding you personally responsible for the safety of these people. You'll see that their movement thrives and prospers."

"What?" O'Brien quivered with indignant fury, mounted the first step to the throne. "They mean to kill you!"

Emperor Movius resumed his seat on his throne. "Of course they do. That's Janus Peterson's worry." He shook his head. "Poor Nate. In spite of all of your charts and figures, the very simple meaning of everything you did has escaped you."

O'Brien folded his arms across his chest. "Really?"

Movius' face grew serious. "Nate, you of all people should see it." He leaned forward, "Fifteen years ago. . .

whenever it was you saw this crisis coming, you decided to take a hand in it. Your motive was preserving your own special knowledge, the cultural data you had accumulated for the use of future generations."

"Yes, but ..."

"Let me finish." Movius leaned back, watching O'Brien carefully. "You took a hand - you looked for the catalyst. Brownley was one who failed. You picked me up back there somewhere, guided, cajoled and tricked me into the crucial position in the revolution. It was revolution—and this is the important point— against the government of which you were a part. You might say you planned to overthrow yourself."

O'Brien took a step toward the throne, waved an angry hand. "You're the one who misses the point. I was trying to preserve something in spite of a revolution that was *inevitably* coming. Inevitably is the important word. There was no chance the government wouldn't be overthrown, I was trying to save ..."

Movius interrupted him. "And what makes you think this will last?" He waved a hand around the throne room, at the gold trappings and ostentation, "How long do you think the people of the world will tolerate me ... or if they don't assassinate me, it will be one of my descendants." He frowned. "Another revolution is even more inevitable than the last one."

O'Brien took another step up toward the throne. "The report from Istanbul could be the faint beginnings of the end for everything you represent."

Movius stood up, looked down on the tiny figure of O'Brien. "Of course it is! That is why you are personally responsible for the safety of those people. We have been fortunate enough to catch the countermovement at the beginning. We can nurture it if we want to preserve whatever is worth saving in our present culture. Do you see my point now?"

O'Brien pulled at his ear. "I think you're out of your mind," he said.

Emperor Movius smiled a grim smile. "The significance of what we have done has been known to many governments, seldom practiced in its pure form."

"Get to the point, will you?" snapped O'Brien.

Emperor Movius ignored the anger of his advisor. He extended his arms regally. "For a civilization to survive a crisis . . . in order that the good will not go with the bad . . . it is essential that an element of the government have charge of the revolution."

About the Author

Frank Herbert, the visionary author of *Dune*, wrote more than twenty other novels, including *Hellstrom's Hive*, *The White Plague*, *The Green Brain*, and *The Dosadi Experiment*. During his life, he received great acclaim for his sweeping vision and the deep philosophical underpinnings in his writings. His life is detailed in the Hugo-nominated biography *Dreamer of Dune*, by Brian Herbert.

Other Frank Herbert novels available from WordFire Press include *Destination: Void*, *The Heaven Makers*, *Direct Descent*, *The Jesus Incident* (with Bill Ransom), and his last-published novel, *Man of Two Worlds*, coauthored with his son Brian Herbert.

CPSIA information can be obtained at www.ICGtesting.com
Printed in the USA
BVOW011007110313

315222BV00014B/545/P